Pemberley to Dublin

A Matchmaker's Journey

Pemberley to Dublin

A Matchmaker's Journey

By

Catherine Hemingway

Also by the Author

The Matchmaker of Pemberley

An Amorous Sequel to All Jane Austen's Novels

Dedication

To my Irish ancestors

"The heart of Ireland can be found in the voices of its poets."

Chapter 1

Some might consider a plain face and aloof manner to be a deficit for a single woman of marriageable age, but the Honourable Miss Catherine Carteret considered it to be her second greatest asset; her first being a brilliant and inquisitive mind that valued scholarship and learning over the rules imposed by society. Fortunately, she was born into wealth and had no requirement to marry which was exactly her intention to never do.

As the firstborn child of Viscount Dalrymple, she enjoyed the privileges of wealth and consequence as well as the support of her rather shy, introverted, intellectual father who recognised the unique qualities of his gifted daughter early in her development. On the other hand, her mother despaired of her daughter's focus on education rather than learning her place in society and eventually finding a suitable match, a priority for any eligible young woman, even if she lacked beauty and was disinterested in fashion and social graces. Her parent's marriage had been one of compromise with each party extracting those necessities from the relationship that would allow them to thrive despite the limitations of the other.

Henry Carteret was born a second son with no prospect of an inheritance and was therefore allowed to pursue his intellectual interests in ancient languages, history, antiquities, and the sciences, with the prospect of creating an endowment at Trinity College in Dublin that would provide him a respectable title as a dean of one of the schools and a means of income. The plan was disrupted when his older brother, William, heir to the estate and an avid horseman, had the misfortune of falling from his horse and breaking his neck in a hunting accident leaving behind his wife, Martha, and a young daughter, Margaret. Henry, a bachelor at the time, inherited the title and was thrust into the role of managing the family estate, Rathclare Hall, and tasked with building the family's wealth and prosperity.

Miss Caroline Walsh was from the Old English landed gentry that had claimed property in Ireland two centuries earlier and built large, prosperous estates, but later fell victim to the vicissitudes of ever-changing laws on the part of the English Parliament that limited the fortunes of both Irish Protestants and Catholics alike. She had determined to leverage her modest dowry and ensure her place in society by means of a well-connected marriage and was abundantly endowed with finely composed features, a graceful figure, and captivating manners which were exceeded only by an acute ambition to achieve social prominence. The shy new viscount was no match for her wiles and quickly fell in line behind a woman quite happy to guide him towards increased wealth and distinction in local society. That he had no special aspirations towards either was of little consequence and so they had settled into their separate roles; he pursued his scholarly interests while she pursued an endless array of prosperous connections and social engagements.

Two years after the birth of their daughter, Catherine, she delivered a son named Charles, thus fulfilling the primary duty of a married woman to produce an heir and secure the longevity of the family line through inheritance. The success and prosperity of her children became the focus of her life. Martha, now widowed, moved to Rathclare Park, a smaller home on the family estate, to raise her daughter but succumbed to a fever when Margaret was eight years old, and the child moved back to Rathclare Hall under the care of her aunt and uncle.

"Catherine, my dear, would it surprise you to learn that you can expect a gentleman caller, a recent acquaintance we made in Bath? Surely you remember Colonel Fitzwilliam who stood up for Sir Thomas Bertram when he married our cousin, Elizabeth Elliot. I have just received a note that he recently arrived in Dublin and plans to call on you tomorrow."

"Of course, I remember him, Mamma, but why do you infer that he will be calling on me? We made his acquaintance at the same time, and I think we may presume he wishes to make a courtesy call on both of us."

"Come, come, my dear Catherine, of course he is calling on you. After all, you were the one who broke from your usual custom by accepting his invitation to dance during the reception we gave at the Royal Crescent, and you engaged in extended conversations with him at several other social gatherings. He was quite attentive to you despite your usual pattern of discouraging suitors with your aloofness and disinterest; it would appear you were not entirely successful at discouraging his attentions. I must say I was greatly relieved that you did not try to make a fool of him when he invited you to dance, and I was surprised you even accepted the offer; I held my breath for fear that you might practice your usual method of discouraging partners by turning the wrong way or stepping on his toes. Really, my dear, you should make more of an effort to encourage eligible suitors."

"Mamma, just because I danced with him once in Bath and found his society agreeable enough to engage in a few interesting conversations, you can hardly consider him to be a suitor let alone infer that his reason for making a social call during his travels has anything at all to do with courtship."

"Catherine, you may say whatever you will, but you cannot deny that by all appearances you enjoyed your conversations with him; he seems genial and well informed, his looks are agreeable, his address impeccable, his manners pleasing, he dresses well, and is very much the gentleman, not to mention the fact that he is the son of an earl. Even your cousin, Elizabeth, remarked on his eligibility and rank despite his being a second son, and I do believe if she had not been cheated out of her inheritance and left in an impoverished state by that scoundrel Sir William Elliot, I venture she might have aimed to secure him for herself."

"Ah yes, a second son, in need of marrying an heiress to ensure his standard of living and guarantee his future. Perhaps we may view him more accurately as just another of society's fortune hunters, but, really, it makes no difference, as you know full well that I have no intention of marrying, so if that is his reason for calling, he will be sorely disappointed to have gone to the bother."

"Catherine, is it too much to ask that you make yourself agreeable, extend basic social courtesies to the gentleman, and be open to his attentions? He does you a great honour by travelling so far to pay a call and I shall not have you spurn him because of your stubborn and obstinate decision to remain single. It is unbecoming an eligible young lady of consequence and you have an obligation to your family to reconcile yourself to the prospect of marriage. If your father were still alive, he would support me on this topic to be sure. He set aside a sizeable dowry for just such a purpose, not to support your life as a spinster, whatever you may think."

"Mamma, at seven and twenty I am well past the courtship years of an 'eligible young lady'. I am committed to my work and my studies, which my father fully approved and supported, and I shall not trade that in to become the possession of a husband and brood mare for a gaggle of children. You know my feelings on this, and I have the means to stand by this decision thanks to my father. Will you please relent on this subject at last? I will happily demonstrate all the necessary courtesies to Colonel Fitzwilliam when he arrives tomorrow as I do find his society agreeable, but you must limit your expectations of that leading to anything more than a friendly exchange of goodwill. He is a man of information and an engaging conversationalist with whom I enjoyed some rather lively discussions when we met in Bath, but that is all you can expect. Does he say what time we may expect him?"

"He will come at teatime in the afternoon, and I admonish you to dress appropriately for our guest. None of this grey you seem to favour these days. Wear the pretty green dress with the lace trim I just had made; it is a becoming colour on you, and have Bridget do your hair up. Really, it is distressing you pay so little attention to your appearance."

What her mother said was quite true. She learned to take advantage of her tall, thin frame, unremarkable complexion, and lank brown hair dressed as unfashionably as her gowns, to go largely unnoticed when she had entered her adolescence and experienced the pressure of the rites of passage associated with becoming an eligible young lady in society. Towards that end she came to realise early on that being a purposefully clumsy dance partner would ensure she was asked infrequently. That she was considered plain of looks, awkward, shy, and aloof added to her coat of armour and discouraged attention from suitors. The more she eschewed the demands made by society the more it freed her to pursue her own interests, which she did with great appetite and relish.

Foremost, she had learned from a very early age that she had a great aptitude for languages. Her first had been learning the local Irish language, a Gaelic dialect, that was forbidden to be spoken by the servants but was used frequently when no one was around to observe it. Her mind was like a sponge, and she learned vocabulary and pronunciation effortlessly which she kept to herself, as it amused her to eavesdrop when she was within hearing of the servants, and only accidentally revealed it to them at the age of four when she asked a question of the maid who was dressing her. Thereafter the staff were careful not to speak it around her, but by then it was too late, and they were far too unobservant to realise when she was nearby, so it became her little secret.

What was not a secret was her precocity for Latin and Greek, languages that her father favoured to study and speak with his friends from Trinity College. While he was now a viscount, he had lost none of his interest and enthusiasm for studying ancient scrolls and antiquities. When he first heard Catherine speak in Latin, he assumed she was merely parroting sounds that she did not understand. When she began to recite passages and ask about their meanings at the age of six, he knew that she was intellectually gifted in a very significant way. It was so remarkable that when his scholarly friends from Trinity came to call, she was invited to demonstrate her proficiency almost as a parlor trick. His friends were amazed and encouraging much to his wife's chagrin, who considered her precocity unseemly and meant to discourage the demonstrations.

By the time she was ten she was conversant in French, Italian, Spanish, and Portuguese along with Greek and Latin. When a visiting German professor came to call, she quickly developed an aptitude for that language as well. She kept the Gaelic as her little secret knowing neither of her parents would approve since it was a forbidden language. Her interests were not limited to languages for, like her father, she loved antiquities and history, including translating manuscripts and annotating scrolls from ancient times. She had an aptitude for the sciences as well and took particular interest in the medicinal use of plants and herbs keeping a personal garden near the kitchen garden.

Her father felt an obligation to allow her to develop her gifts and was relieved when his son reached an age so that officially engaging a tutor would be tolerated by his wife without disquieting her, thus giving him an opening to include Catherine in the lessons. Lady Dalrymple much preferred to have her daughter focus on learning music, drawing or watercolour taught by highly trained masters, as well as the finer points of sewing, needle point, and country dances alongside other young ladies her age. The French language and even a little Italian were acceptable to demonstrate a worldly education, but Catherine's natural facility on that front far exceeded those of any local teacher. Calling on neighbours and receiving guests was another of her mother's priorities in which Catherine grudgingly participated. Conversation about the weather and roads, the latest fashions, upcoming balls, social excursions, and teas, all were tedious, unwelcome events, and a distraction from her studies. At her father's insistence, she was allowed to join her brother and his tutor in the mornings before her mother demanded her daughter's time for the rest of the day.

Her brother had neither her drive nor appetite for studies being rambunctious by nature and easily distracted.

Conjugating Latin verbs and translating simple sentences seemed a worthless occupation to Charles who far preferred outdoor activities like riding, hunting, and fishing. He displayed all the airs of a traditional country gentleman matched by a natural amiability that made him widely admired in social circles. Taking after his mother, his pleasing countenance and agreeable address ensured the attention of many highly eligible young ladies and when he came of age, his father had arranged a match with Augusta Byrne, a socially prominent descendant of an Old English, Protestant family long established as large estate owners near Dublin, who was perfectly suited to marry Charles and carry on the family dynasty.

Much to her mother-in-law's delight, Augusta was predisposed to enjoy the role of a leading socialite who eagerly engaged in planning and participating in events that her sister-in-law abhorred. She had a large coterie of friends and delighted in identifying eligible suitors and plotting matches that would advance the social standing of those closest to her, requiring her to stay abreast of all the latest news and gossip which she did with relish. When her father-in-law fell ill and passed away unexpectedly, she enthusiastically embraced the role of Viscountess Dalrymple along with her young husband, Charles, and fulfilled her duty by providing two sons, William and Henry, now aged 7 and 5.

* ~ * ~ * ~ *

When the housekeeper announced the arrival of Colonel

Fitzwilliam and showed him into the drawing room, Lady Dalrymple welcomed him and immediately sent for Catherine. She was met with a bow and an amiable smile by the gentleman; his face reflecting the healthy glow of exercise, the aftermath of having arrived on horseback, and exhibiting the relaxed, affable goodwill that seemed to permeate all his social encounters.

"How kind of you to call on us, Colonel Fitzwilliam. We are delighted to see you, are we not, Catherine?" said the viscountess with far more warmth and enthusiasm than she usually demonstrated towards new acquaintances.

"Yes, Mamma," replied Catherine with an edge of impatience in her voice. "May I ask what brings you to Dublin, Colonel? Are you here on business or leisure pursuits?"

"I have a great affection for Ireland and make it a practice to visit as often as I can. I was stationed in Dublin in 1796 when there were concerns about the arrival of a French fleet to support a Catholic uprising, and the experience stirred my fascination with the locale and its residents. Dublin is one of the most splendid capitols in northern Europe with its great courtyards and buildings; Trinity College and College Green; the grandeur of the Parliament building outshines its rival in London, in my opinion; and the Royal Exchange, Four Courts with its dome and rotunda, the Dame Street theatre district, all make for compelling reasons to visit. I find the wide streets and squares are much to be admired with assorted bridges and walkways along the banks of the Liffey. Politicians and professors, merchants and sailors, actors and musicians, fashionable gentlemen and ladies are all to be found here. I was recently told that the heart of Ireland can be found in the voices of its poets, and I have a great fondness for poetry," he replied with the slightest of smiles and a nod to Catherine.

"Do tell us news of our new acquaintances in Bath. We were ever so pleased to attend the engagement party of your cousin, Miss Darcy, to Dr. James Baldwin. Have their nuptials taken place since last we met?" asked the viscountess. "They were such a delightful young couple. I have always maintained that marriage brings great felicity to both families while the newlyweds emit a special radiance that emanates to all in their orbit; indeed, the blessings of marriage are considerable, would you agree, Colonel?"

"Indeed," he replied. "My darling cousin, Georgianna, and Dr. Baldwin took their vows at the family estate of Pemberley in Derbyshire earlier this month and it was a joyous occasion. In fact, the true felicity to which you refer extended its reach to another young couple, Mrs. Darcy's sister, Miss Kitty Bennet; she became engaged to Mr. Thomas Baldwin, the brother of the groom, to the delight of all the families involved. It was announced just prior to the wedding and the new Mrs. Baldwin will now have a permanent connection with her dearest friend, Miss Bennet, as her future sister-in-law, and both will reside near each other in Bath. It seems marriage may have been a contagious element in that fair city when you consider the courtship and marriage of Sir Thomas Bertram to your cousin, Miss Elizabeth Elliot, followed shortly by the engagements of the Misses Darcy and Bennet."

"How delightful!" exclaimed the viscountess. "What a

happy outcome for all, do you not agree, Catherine? Indeed, who knows what might follow should the marriage contagion continue to spread beyond Bath," smiled her mother.

"I am certain there are some who must have immunity from such a contagion, Mamma," replied her daughter, while making a concerted effort to conceal her perturbation with her mother for encouraging and prolonging this line of conversation. While Colonel Fitzwilliam's presence was not unwelcome, this point of discussion and her mother's enthusiasm for the topic was.

Perhaps sensing her sentiments, the colonel suggested that he would take great pleasure in seeing the grounds of the estate if Miss Carteret was agreeable to guiding the tour. "I remember hearing from Lady Bertram that during her stay, you took much pleasure in walking in the gardens and did so often. I would greatly enjoy a tour if you're amenable to the idea of an outing?"

"Of course, Catherine, you must extend the courtesy of a tour of the grounds to Colonel Fitzwilliam," exhorted her mother. "It is such a lovely day, you should enjoy the favourable weather, and I will have tea served when you return from your walk. Do take your time for there is no hurry on my account."

With relief Catherine acquiesced to the scheme, donning a straw bergère with green ribbons and proceeded from the drawing room through a door that led outside to a large garden that was immaculately manicured with hedges enclosing flowers, separated by brick walkways leading to a small pond and beyond that an open woodland.

"May I ask how long since you arrived in Dublin?" asked Catherine.

"Just a few days ago. It has been almost two years since my last visit, and I felt a desire to reacquaint myself with the country. I have plans to travel south to Waterford and then west to Connacht. I have a longing to visit Waterford Glassworks which is said to create the finest quality crystal in the world, and I understand touring the facility is quite a remarkable experience; I greatly enjoy observing artisans at work and I am interested in the manufacturing process that combines flint and crown glass to enhance the optical properties of both; science and art working together.

"I have you to thank for my interest in visiting Connacht after being schooled in the existence of an Irish pirate queen and her negotiations with Queen Elizabeth more than two centuries ago. I am quite intrigued to hear the folklore and learn more of the history behind the story of Grace O'Malley. I consider it a worthwhile undertaking to pursue the legend of such an adventurous female buccaneer and shall report back to you on any salacious intrigues that I happen to uncover if you like?"

"I am all astonishment that my revealing the story of Grace O'Malley had such an impact on you, Colonel, especially to have inspired an adventurous journey to such a remote place. Shall I take care to guard against sharing other historical records with you lest you feel compelled to rush off on impetuous quests for information on little-known characters in history?"

"Indeed, I hope you do continue sharing such anecdotes as

will inspire my appetite for adventure. I should be vastly disappointed if you withheld these intriguing references that are so readily at hand to you as a student of history. From whence is your interest derived? It is unusual to find such a well-educated woman as you and I wonder at the source of your studies and exposure to subjects such as history. Were you introduced to science and mathematics as well? Languages perhaps?"

"My father was a gifted intellectual and linguist closely associated with Trinity College and promoted my education from an early age when he discovered I had a unique facility for languages. Although education was frowned upon for young ladies, as we are expected to be docile, obedient, fragile things dependent on men, he recognised that my unusual gifts deserved development, much to my mother's vexation.

"She was adamant that my brother and I both be instructed in manners, speech, dress, and dance, but from there our paths were to diverge. He was to be taught science, mathematics, arts, language, and literature while my focus was to be on making myself pleasing to potential suitors and minimising my educational pursuits which were considered unattractive and unwarranted. As I was no beauty and eager to learn, I resisted the direction given by my mother, and my father, who took pity on my plight, arranged for me to join my brother in studies when a tutor was brought in to advance his education. My father interceded with my mother to ensure my mornings were dedicated to learning and my afternoons devoted to living up to her expectations, as well as those of society at large, as evidenced by the ceaseless visits between neighbours, endless dinners, entertainments, and balls. I was highly successful in my educational endeavours and managed to subvert my mother's goals whenever possible."

"A subversive!" he laughed. "How intriguing. I must confess my great curiosity as to ways by which you subverted your mother's efforts to promote you in society. Did you take to your bed and refuse to socialise? How does one conspire to elude these demands for I have often wished to avoid such tedious occurrences myself?"

"By performing all the tasks as poorly as possible, of course, for that is the key," she laughed. "For instance, if you step on enough toes or turn the wrong way in a dance set, you will eventually stop being invited to dance and perhaps be fortunate enough to find your way to the library or study."

"Am I fortunate that you did not subject me to this devious device when I invited you to dance at the reception in Bath where first we met? You danced quite well and were a charming partner which makes me wonder what compelled you to accept my offer?"

"Once I determined to accept your invitation, I made the decision not to embarrass you with unprovoked mistakes meant to discourage you, as it seemed unjustifiable under the circumstances, since you had no way of knowing this was my usual strategy to discourage dance partners. I was surprised when you approached me as I make it a habit to remain as aloof as possible in such settings, and I wondered what motivated you to extend the invitation. Also, my mother would have been terribly vexed if I had embarrassed her at the reception since she was hosting it; I am sure she was excessively concerned that I might do something imprudent from the moment we joined the dance set until it finished."

"Then I shall consider myself lucky to have avoided an embarrassing moment. As to the impetus to extend the invitation, I was curious about your disposition as I had heard of rather ungenerous comments made about you by your cousin, Miss Elizabeth Elliot, Lady Bertram that is, whom your mother had kindly taken under wing after the death of her father. I was merely curious to determine if your diffidence was imagined or if you had been judged unfairly."

"Do you think you can apprehend one's character in the short interval of a country dance?" she asked.

"Perhaps not your full character but I found your conversation as candid as it was amusing, which was unexpected and refreshing, and you did dance very well might I add."

Catherine managed a small nod of approval and with that they adjourned their discussion to rejoin her mother in the drawing room where tea was being served. As they took their seats there was a noise in the entryway and the housekeeper opened the door followed by the extravagant entrance of a handsome, elegant young woman of graceful bearing who enthusiastically declared, "Dear Mamma, have you heard the latest news of our neighbours, the Brennans? It is quite unexpected I assure you and I wasted not a moment to drop in since I was passing by anyway. Oh dear, my apologies, for I did not know you were receiving guests this afternoon, and a gentleman caller no less. Another unexpected event but most highly welcomed I can assure you. Please forgive the intrusion; I do hope I am not interrupting anything private."

"Colonel Fitzwilliam, may I introduce you to my daughter-in-law, the Viscountess Dalrymple. Augusta, Colonel Edward Fitzwilliam is a new acquaintance we met in Bath on our last visit, and it happens that he stood up for Sir Thomas Bertram when he married our cousin Elizabeth. He recently arrived in Dublin and has just now made a call on us."

Catherine's discomfort at the unexpected arrival of her sister-in-law at this inauspicious moment was exceeded only by her concern that this notorious busybody would not only jump to conclusions about the intentions of the new visitor but insinuate more to the connection than the visit merited. While she always enjoyed her conversations with the colonel and his presence was not unwelcome, she wanted no conjectures on the part of her family as to the motives of his visit or his intentions as they pertained to her. This was equally true regarding him; whatever his purposes were for travelling to Ireland, she wanted no misapprehensions about her interest in him beyond a casual acquaintanceship.

"What an unexpected delight it is to have a gentleman caller visiting my sister-in-law. I marvel at my excellent timing. May I ask how long you'll be visiting in our fair city, sir?" asked Augusta.

"I have no set time for my visit but do plan a few sojourns to other parts of the country including Waterford," replied Edward.

"Waterford! How lovely. I have become quite attached to the cut-glass bowl my husband gave me for our anniversary. It is quite spectacular you know. You remember the one,

Mamma, I used it to serve punch at Easter when we had the large gathering, and I must say our guests were very impressed with its size and brilliancy, and the dear little serving cups are so delightful to hold. I received ever so many compliments, and we were quite the envy of all our friends I can assure you. You must pay a visit upon your return, Colonel, and report all you learn about the craftsmanship as I am sure my husband, the viscount, will be eager to hear about it; he is excessively interested in all the finest of amenities for entertaining. What an amusing scheme you already have planned for your travels, and I can assure you my husband will be delighted to meet you and learn more of your plans.

"In fact, I stopped by to invite dear Mamma and Catherine to dine with us tomorrow after church. You must promise to join them! I'm sure I can think of nothing that would please my husband more than to make your acquaintance. You can tell us all about our cousin's new husband, Sir Thomas Bertram, a baronet no less. Indeed, imagine our delight when we learned of Elizabeth's marriage; I knew that eventually she would enchant someone of rank who would wish to marry such an elegant creature. We had hoped she might find a match during her visit here, even though she was in mourning at the time, but alas, no one quite suited her from amongst our acquaintances, and to think it all happened so quickly; they knew each other for just a month or more. Imagine that? Still, where romance is concerned, time is of no matter, do you not agree? No matter whatsoever. Well, I must be off. Please promise to join us tomorrow, Colonel. I will save my news about the Brennans for later, Mamma. Until tomorrow." With that Viscountess Dalrymple swept out of the house with a flourish.

Catherine was severely importuned by the entire direction of the conversation and immediately asserted to Colonel Fitzwilliam that he was under no obligation to accept the invitation. She could already foresee her family becoming attached to the notion that his purpose in visiting included courtship and wished to suppress any such extraordinary ideas by all parties involved. She shrank from the idea of extending his acquaintance further than it was already established which could be considered superficial at best.

"We have no wish to interfere with the schemes you may already have designed for tomorrow, Colonel, and you are certainly under no obligation to accommodate my sister-in-law's invitation considering how unexpectedly it surfaced. Please do not hesitate to decline the offer if you are so inclined so you may pursue your original plans unencumbered, as I am sure my brother and his wife will understand."

"My dear, your words could be considered impolitic for you are in danger of making our guest feel most unwelcomed which I am sure cannot be your intention," said Lady Dalrymple to her daughter with a raise of her eyebrows as well as her voice.

"Of course, we would be greatly obliged if you choose to join us tomorrow, Colonel, and I am sure you will be highly gratified to make the acquaintance of my son who is a most charming gentleman and to see the family estate which is quite impressive you know and is much admired. We attend Christ Church services at 11:00 a.m. and can arrange to pick you up in our carriage after the service. Dinner is served early on Sundays as it is necessary to give the servants' time to themselves later in the day. Some of them are Catholics you know, and I am sure find their way to Papist services where they may, but we must tolerate it as it is difficult to find good Protestant servants for all positions although we do make the effort. Please say you will join us as your companionship will be most welcomed by all of us."

Colonel Fitzwilliam replied that he was delighted to receive the invitation and not at all indisposed to accept it as he had no pressing plans for the next day and would greatly enjoy a visit to the family seat and a view of the countryside. "I am quite fond of walking and the church is within easy reach of my accommodations; I relish a morning stroll and will plan to meet you at the end of the service if that is agreeable, so long as it does not importune Miss Carteret for whom, it seems, the entire plan was unanticipated. Perhaps she had other designs for how she would spend her day."

"I can assure you that it will do my daughter a great deal of good to spend a pleasant afternoon with family and friends rather than locked away in her study as is her usual habit. We shall look for you after the service and arrange for you to join us in our carriage. I am sure you will have a most amusing time, and we will gladly welcome your company for the afternoon, do you not agree, Catherine?"

Chapter 2

"Such an honour to have you in attendance at our service, Viscount Dalrymple," exclaimed Reverend Murray as he vigorously shook his hand. "I do hope you approved of the sermon today, after all, we are the beneficiary of your inestimable generosity. Indeed, we would be unable to continue our ongoing work identifying gifted pupils from necessitous Catholic families for scholarships to attend our Protestant Charter Schools. The hedge schools are a scandal but so difficult to stamp out even though they are outlawed, and yet Catholics must receive an education if they are to contribute to society. What better solution than removing the students from their families so they can be educated as Protestants and become advocates for the Church of Ireland? We are in your debt for supporting this vital and worthy cause."

"Yes, of course," replied the viscount, as he extracted his hand from the grip of the rector. "We must all do our part to support the spread of the true faith and allow worthy students to better themselves. Keep up the good work, Mr. Murray."

"Viscountess, to have you in attendance on such a glorious day is a blessing indeed, and may I be so bold as to say your mere presence elevates the observance of our Lord's Day to even greater grandeur," enthused Reverend Murray bowing deeply to Augusta as she passed with a nod.

"Good day to you, Dowager Viscountess. May the blessings of the Lord be with you, and may he hold your beloved husband close to the bosom of his heart. I believe a better man never lived than your dear, departed, husband and you must consider your own sorrow as a mere shadow of the joy with which he was received in heaven. Such felicity to have you among us today; may you be rewarded with good health for the rest of your days. And whom have we here but your charming daughter, the Honourable Miss Carteret, gracing our service. Such a privilege to have you both here today," he continued to prattle as the dowager acknowledge him with a smile and Catherine gave him a diffident look.

Throughout the service Catherine wondered if Colonel Fitzwilliam was in attendance or still planning to join them for the afternoon. She was vexed by her family for swooping in to include him in their party and discomfited by the prospect of spending time with a man whom she admired for his amiable qualities and lively conversation yet felt intruded upon by his very presence in their midst and the pressures she could see building in the mindset of her family. It was too much to bear and caused a great disturbance to her tranquillity; she had created an orderly life for herself to pursue her interests and, heretofore, managed to regulate her family's expectations about her future and her decision to never marry. This unplanned disruption was an irritant and a distraction even though it reflected no ill will towards the source of the disturbance.

As they extricated themselves from the obsequious pastor and moved towards the exit Catherine spied Colonel Fitzwilliam standing near a tree on the grounds of the church looking relaxed and genial, exuding good-humour and confidence. He caught her glance and gave her a nod of recognition before stepping forward to join her party. Introductions ensued and the exaggerated enthusiasm of her brother and his wife as well as her mother left her with an urge to flee the churchyard and abandon them all to their shameless opportunism at her expense. Not that she blamed the colonel who was an unwitting victim of their presumptuous behaviour; nevertheless, his presence had stirred up a tempest of upheaval in her otherwise tranquil world. As there was no escaping her conspiratorial family, she was determined to conceal her vexation knowing that the visitor would soon begin his journey of discovery to other parts of the country and no longer importune her or invigorate false notions of future connections within her family.

Upon their arrival at Rathclare Hall, the family seat, and following a tour of the splendid estate and a discussion of the heredity of the Dalrymple family in Ireland with their connection to the first Earl of Stair in Scotland, the party was seated in the large dining room for the repast when Charles asked Colonel Fitzwilliam about his travel plans.

"I understand from my wife that you have visited our fair country before, Colonel, and that you have plans to travel to the south. I believe Waterford is one of your destinations. Is that what brings you to our shores or are there larger plans at work?" asked Charles, casting a knowing smile to Augusta that made Catherine want to cringe.

"I have several areas of interest during my travels," replied Colonel Fitzwilliam. "I am eager to visit the Trinity College Library in hopes of seeing the historic *Book of Kells* which I understand is on display there. I am told it is regarded as a national treasure and was put in safekeeping at the college around 1653, but more recently was made available for public viewing. It is said they are uniquely illustrated with brilliant colours, ornate Celtic knots, and images of mythical beasts. That such precious manuscripts have survived to this day is a very compelling reason to make a special trip to see them."

"Then you are in luck, my good man. Seated next to you is the key to unlocking your private viewing experience for not only does my sister have access to the guardians of these manuscripts you seek, but she is also fluent in Latin and can even serve as your interpreter when viewing them if needed. She is an expert in antiquities and has many associates at Trinity who rely on her abilities. She knows Greek as well, do you not, Catherine?"

"Yes," replied Catherine to her brother with a note of exasperation in her voice. Then softening, she directed her attention to the visitor and went on to say she would be happy to arrange a special viewing of the treasured manuscripts during her next visit to the college. "I am sure you will find it a worthwhile application of your time if it does not interfere with your trip to Waterford and journey to Connacht."

"I have no specific time in mind for my journey other than waiting for fair weather when I sail to Waterford and then on to Connacht. My plans are entirely flexible and if I may have the privilege of escorting you to Trinity College and relying on your unique insights, I am certain to learn more with you by my side. I am at your service whenever you wish. You may name the day."

"May I ask what takes you to Connacht?" interjected Viscount Dalrymple. "Waterford in the south has its attractions but the west of Ireland is extremely poor, rather wild I'm afraid, and overrun with Papists who have no love for the British. Surely there can be little of interest to attract you to such an outpost as Connacht."

"Then perhaps you have not heard of Grace O'Malley, the Pirate Queen of Connacht," replied Colonel Fitzwilliam.

Silence followed this announcement momentarily until finally the dowager viscountess, on observing a small smile cross her daughter's face, spoke up. "Pray tell me your trip is not based on some outlandish story told to you by my daughter, Colonel. She will make a knowledgeable guide at Trinity College to see the *Book of Kells* for she is well known and admired there by colleagues of my dear departed husband, but you must consider some of the stories she comes across may be far-fetched and anecdotal at best. I caution you to not subscribe to all the wild tales she comes across in her research, for the western seas are rough and there are few attractions once you arrive in such an outback place. There may be pirates in the region to this day!"

"Mamma, the story of Grace O'Malley is documented not only in Ireland but also in England as it is well known she met with Queen Elizabeth to negotiate the release of her son. I happened to share her history with Colonel Fitzwilliam while we were in Bath and apparently it captured his imagination; that it spurred his interest to visit Connacht is entirely his own doing," replied Catherine.

"Ah, you make it sound like a risky and perilous adventure indeed," he answered, "which intrigues me all the more and further excites my interest to embark on this quest but, let me assure you, I will not be travelling alone and have engaged able-bodied men to accompany me and guarantee my safety, if I find myself confronted with treacherous inhabitants or seafaring pirates. I plan to sail the eastern coast to Waterford as I've only seen a portion of it, from there south to Bantry Bay and then on to the western shore to see the Cliffs of Moher which I'm told are very impressive, and from there on to Connacht. I have spent time in Dublin over the years and visited north to Belfast, but this will give me a better view of the entire country, the beauty of which I already greatly admire."

"Pray tell us what you expect to find in Connacht?" asked Charles. "Surely memories of this pirate queen from over two hundred years ago will be long since lost to folklore. What can there be to discover? Certainly not pirate gold or the spoils of stolen treasure. Such a journey seems a fool's errand if you will forgive my saying so. If it is adventure you like, you will certainly find it on your journey, but it is a long way to travel in search of intelligence on the existence of a long-lost pirate queen. Did you say Grace O'Malley was her name? To be sure, every soul you meet in Connacht will claim to be an O'Malley descendant once they see a fine British gentleman making inquiries."

"Perhaps you will be right," laughed Fitzwilliam, "but my sense of adventure drives me on and why not make an expedition to view your beautiful country from the sea, and uncover local lore along the way, be it in Waterford or Connacht? I expect to have many tales of my journey and will gladly share them with you upon my return."

Catherine was relieved when the conversation turned to other topics as she felt certain that her mother would harp on the subject later and scold her for setting the idea in motion. Still, she had to admire the aplomb of Colonel Fitzwilliam who managed the entire incident with his usual ease, poise, and composure.

Chapter 3

The day had arrived for the visit to view the *Book of Kells* at the Trinity College library. Catherine was scheduled to return some Greek manuscripts she had been appending to Edmund Fitzgerald, the Dean of the College of Theology and head of Ancient Languages and Antiquities. She had prearranged to pick up Colonel Fitzwilliam at his lodgings, much to her mother's chagrin.

"Are you prepared to ruin your good name and that of your family?" demanded her mother. "It is positively scandalous for you to ride alone in a carriage with Colonel Fitzwilliam even if it is only a short ride to the college. What can you be thinking?"

"I have long since forsaken any notion of impropriety regarding my comings and goings at the college, Mother, and you know that. I am twenty and seven, well past my formative years, and have been making these trips, unattended, to see Dean Fitzgerald ever since father died. What possible difference can it make for the colonel to ride with me? I am sure our acquaintances have completely lost interest in my comings and goings at the college and if they have not, let them impugn me as they will. I have no intention of giving up my work with Dean Fitzgerald, who is old enough to be my father," replied Catherine.

"Surely the colonel could meet you there rather than riding in the carriage with you unattended?"

"Really, Mamma. It is far more convenient to drive him to our destination than searching for him once I arrive, and he can help carry the manuscripts that I am returning. If people choose to gossip about my independence, let them, for it matters not one whit to me, and I beg your forbearance in this matter."

"Well then, take Bridget with you if you need help with the manuscripts," insisted her mother.

"I will not take my maid with me and that is final," declared Catherine emphatically.

Colonel Fitzwilliam was waiting outside when the carriage pulled up and immediately joined her. "Thank you for offering the ride although it would have been perfectly agreeable for me to meet you there and I do hope riding alone with me will not be considered a breach of decorum by your acquaintances; I am loath to do anything that would impugn your reputation."

"Be not alarmed about damaging my reputation, Colonel. I

can assure you that I have long since breached the boundaries of propriety with my solitary visits to the college. I used to accompany my father to visit his colleagues and have continued to do so since his death bearing the stigma of my unconventional behaviour with pride. I will not be importuned by rumourmongers and have no qualms about raising the suspicions of local gossips by riding in the carriage with you," she replied with a smile. "I look forward to showing you the library which cannot help but impress. It dates back to 1732 with the Long Room measuring some 65 metres long and housing tens of thousands of books and manuscripts. My dear friend, Dean Edmund Fitzgerald, is a delight and the most well-informed historian you will ever have the pleasure of meeting. His expansive knowledge of ancient languages and antiquities is exceeded only by the unabashed delight he takes when expounding on those subjects, for he is quite a fascinating man despite his years and charms everyone with whom he comes in contact."

"My dear, Catherine, how good it is to see you, and this must be the gentleman you mentioned in your note. Welcome to Trinity, sir. Welcome, indeed! You could not find a more accomplished companion to showcase our library than the honourable Miss Carteret who is a highly esteemed scholar amongst our elite circle of historians and theologians; none better including myself mind you. Such a facility for languages! It's quite remarkable, even when she was a little girl," gushed Dean Fitzgerald whose rosy round face was ebullient with pleasure.

Catherine's cheeks coloured as she spoke; "Dean Fitzgerald, may I introduce Colonel Fitzwilliam, a recent acquaintance I met during a visit to Bath who has just arrived for a tour of Ireland and expressed a wish to view the *Book of Kells* while visiting our fair city. Since I just finished annotating the transcription of the Augustinian manuscript you requested and was preparing to return it to you, I invited him to join me for a tour. I do hope our visit does not importune you?"

"Oh my, no. You are always welcome as is any friend of yours who fancies to engage in a dialogue about our greatest of medieval treasures, miraculously preserved over the centuries. Come, let us commence. When it is on public display it is open only to a single illuminated page, but you shall see all four gospels and the superb illustrations within."

They entered a small windowless room lined with bookshelves featuring a glass cabinet on a small, stone table illuminated from above by a series of suspended lanterns at one end of the room, with an opening in a wall where the famed *Book of Kells* could be viewed through a sliding partition from a larger room on the other side. The book was opened to a folio featuring an illuminated image which was extraordinary for the brilliancy of the colours and intricacy of design.

Dean Fitzgerald explained, "Here you see what many consider to be the chief treasure of the western world, the magnificent *Book of Kells*. The page currently on view is The Chi Rho introducing Matthew's account of the nativity and is the single most famous page in medieval art for its incomparable illustrations. The ornamentation is of such extraordinary fineness and delicacy that the artist's skills have been likened to those of a goldsmith."

Colonel Fitzwilliam gasped with amazement and marvelled at the sumptuousness of the beautiful images before him. "How many artists were involved, do you think?" he asked.

"There were three artists in all that created the major decorated pages," the dean answered, then, donning white gloves he removed the treasure from the glass cabinet and began slowly and carefully turning pages of the folios explaining as he went. "Here we see symbols of the evangelists representing Matthew as the Man, Mark as the Lion, Luke as the Calf, and John as the Eagle. These are narrative scenes representing the arrest of Christ here, and his temptation by the Devil as you see here. Then we have portraits of Matthew and John, but there are none of Mark or Luke, at least that have survived."

"Such intricate, interwoven Celtic knotwork motifs around the portraits of the evangelists," observed Colonel Fitzwilliam. "What type of materials did they use?"

"The codex is written on both sheepskin and vellum," replied Catherine. "The whiter vellum was used for the ornamentation and the more mottled sheepskin for the script. Four major scribes copied the text into folios that form the larger volumes. Unfortunately, around 30 folios went missing during the medieval and early modern periods."

"When was the book originally created and how did it come to be here at Trinity College?" asked Fitzwilliam.

"We cannot be sure. A monastery founded by St. Columcille on Iona was raided by Vikings in 806 and the Columban monks sought refuge in a new monastery at Kells in county Meath. There is no way of knowing if the book was produced wholly at Iona or at Kells, or partially at each location. Following the rebellion of 1641, the church at Kells lay in ruins and around 1653 the book was sent to Dublin by the governor of Kells, and it has since resided here at Trinity," answered the dean.

When the sacred treasure was returned to its place under the glass cabinet, the three adjourned to Dean Fitzgerald's office where he and Catherine discussed the writings of Augustine of Hippo while Colonel Fitzwilliam listened on with great admiration. Clearly the dean had a great deal of admiration for the knowledge exhibited by Miss Carteret, whom he had known from a tender age reciting Latin passages at the knee of her father.

* ~ * ~ * ~ *

"What an extraordinary experience," enthused the colonel as they climbed into the carriage and began the drive back towards his lodgings. "Before I arrived, I hoped to merely view a notable historical treasure and admire its beauty from afar like any other visitor. Thanks to you, I was privileged to not only see this incomparable, illustrated masterpiece up close, but also to learn about its unique history from two remarkable experts. Dean Fitzgerald is a delightful acquaintance, generous with his time and expertise, and clearly a great admirer of yours. How shall I repay such a service?"

"If you are willing to take the risk and engage in a rather subversive plan that would shock and dismay my mother, I should like to visit a pub. I have always longed to hear local fiddlers, poets, and singers, gathered to share a pint and their stories with their friends and neighbours, and I may never get such an opportunity again. Will you grant me this indulgence?"

A stunned Colonel Fitzwilliam burst into laughter. "At the risk of never being allowed to cross the thresholds of your mother's or your brother's homes, how can I deny you? Surely your family will consider it a great transgression, a slur on the family name, and it will put me at great risk of never being allowed to call on you again or relay the stories of the adventures I am about to embark on to Waterford and Connacht."

Catherine smiled and conspiratorially whispered, "Then we must keep it our secret for I do not wish to obviate the pleasure of hearing the tales of your voyage with all the inherent risks and hazards, considering that I am at least partially responsible for your quest." She arched an eyebrow waiting for his answer.

He grinned in response and said, "I know a lively place just across from my accommodations, a gathering place for gentry and common folk alike, but safe from unsavoury scoundrels and reprobates. It is a favourite of locals and women are known to join the merrymaking as well. It may be rough and rowdy for your tastes and you must be prepared to quaff a pint of ale if you wish to fit in, unless you have a taste for Irish whiskey instead."

"Guinness is a notable brewery and a great contributor to the prosperity of Dublin including the restoration of St. Patrick's Cathedral. I shall be happy to have a taste of the 'black gold'."

When the new arrivals entered the Gerty Browne, the otherwise lively establishment was temporarily hushed as the colonel and his tall, fashionably attired companion appeared. The highly polished wooden bar extended from a wall into a large, old, but well-appointed room filled with patrons on stools at the bar, in worn upholstered booths, and seated at long tables with benches or at small round tables with wooden chairs. As they took a seat at a table near a window, the fiddler picked up his tune again and the din of conversation was restored. A wide-eyed barmaid approached to take their order and appraise the unusual couple in their midst.

"Good day to you, sir. Tis me honour to be serving yourself and the lady so what's your pleasure?" After receiving the order, she returned shortly gripping two pints of the local favourite stout in her hand.

"Slàinte," said Fitzwilliam as he raised his glass to which Catherine responded in kind. Her eyes were bright with excitement as she took in their surroundings. The din in the room increased as one patron after another spontaneously broke into song and others joined in. As soon as one song finished another began, or someone stood up to recite a favourite poem extolling the ancient exploits of Queen Medb and battles won by her champion, the boy Cuchulainn, with bawdy verses to make any listener blush.

When a lull occurred, a patron at the bar was heard to say, "Gerty, give us another pint and a song if you please."

"And I will gladly take payment for your last pint if you please," replied Gerty who was tending the bar.

"Aye, Gerty. You know meself good for it at the end of the week. Now be a good lass, pour me another pint, and sing us a song for there's none amongst us can carry a tune so well as you. Sing about the Irish Lacemaker."

Others in the room joined in to clamour for a song until finally Gerty relented. She was a small, stout, middle-aged woman with round, rosy cheeks and greying hair. As the proprietess, she was in command of the bar as well as her strong mezzo soprano voice and began singing acapella, filling the room with her sound.

"Once I was young and pretty,
Blue eyes with dark brown hair
Fair of face I moved with grace,
Living life without a care.
"I met an Irish silkie,
Who swore he'd love me true,
He married me and gave to me,
Three bairns who love me too.
"My silkie went a roamin',
My bairns are now full grown,
Tis blessed I was to realise,
My life was now my own.
"I became a fine lacemaker,

Learned at my mother's knee,
I made a start to create the art,
My mother taught to me.
"My beauty now is faded,
My hair is grey and snarled,
But I make my lace with a smiling face,
Though my hands be old and gnarled.
"My journey's almost over,
'Tis advice I will impart,
To play your part with a joyful heart
Make your life a work of art."

The crowd joined in to repeat the last line of her song and roared their approval as she finished with her face wreathed in a smile and taking the slightest of bows before raising her hand dismissively. "Who else can offer us some entertainment? Make yourself heard, tis a boisterous crowd here eager to be pleased," Gerty shouted out.

Catherine, who had been quietly sipping her stout and responding to the atmosphere and liveliness of the crowd, slowly stood up, much to the amazement of every person in the room, none more than Colonel Fitzwilliam. To the shock of all, she began a recitation in the native Irish language which brought a hush to the room, for none expected to hear the words from such an elite, aristocratic woman. They were in her thrall as she spoke in a clear, clarion voice, her head held high, her complexion flushed, speaking the forbidden language of their ancestors. No one in the room listening to her would ever think her features plain or her manner aloof, especially her escort, Colonel Fitzwilliam. When she finished and sat down, the crowd erupted with applause and murmurs arose while many of the men in the audience stood up, doffed their hats, and approached respectfully to say, "Go raibh maith agat," Gaelic for 'thank you' as the colonel later learned.

When they returned to her carriage, Colonel Fitzwilliam expressed his surprise, admiration, and curiosity. "What did you recite?" he inquired. "I've never seen a crowd of people so enthralled."

"Brigid of Kildaire was a famous and pious noblewoman who converted to Catholocism and began her own monastery, after defying her tyrant father who had offered her as wife to a local king. She became an abbess and some say she was even consecrated as a bishop and practiced priestly duties. I recited the table grace used at her monestary as it seemed to suit a place where food and drink are served. I heard it spoken by some of the servants who worked in our kitchen when I first learned their native language. I'll recite it for you so you can understand.

"I should like a great lake of finest ale
For the King of kings
I should like a table of the choicest food
For the family of heaven.
Let the ale be made from the fruits of faith,
And the food be forgiving love.
"I should welcome the poor to my feast,
For they are God's children.
I should welcome the sick to my feast,
For they are God's joy.
Let the poor sit with Jesus at the highest place,

And the sick dance with the angels.
"God bless the poor.
God bless the sick.
And bless our human race.
God bless our food.
God bless our drink,
All homes, O God, embrace."

"Such an apt choice, 'a lake of the finest ale'. No wonder so many stepped forward to thank you when you finished. I am sure it was the last thing they ever expected to hear, and you were the last person they ever would have expected to recite it. You are truly the most amazing woman of my acquaintance, and I will never forget this most memorable of days, having both seen the *Book of Kells* followed by a trip to the local pub to hear you recite a blessing in a forbidden language. 'A lake of finest ale' was inspired."

With that they parted ways and Catherine sat back in the carriage to enjoy her ebullient spirits all the way back to the estate where she held her secret adventure close from the onslaught of inquiries her mother made about the excursion to Trinity College with Colonel Fitzwilliam.

Chapter 4

"You've a sparkle in your eye, Miss and I can't help but wonder was it the rendezvous with the colonel at Trinity that put a rose in your cheeks?" smiled Bridget as she slowly brushed Catherine's long silky hair. "Your mam is still most displeased you went alone, yet you seem happier than ever I've seen you. What is it put's that smile on your face? A certain gentleman?"

"Colonel Fitzwilliam was an excessively good escort, a most intelligent man, and, as it turns out, a willing co-conspirator for my plan. After we left Trinity, I pressed him to take me to a lively pub for a pint of ale and to mingle with the locals! If Mamma was already displeased about the visit to the library she would be doubly displeased to learn I visited a pub."

A look of shock crossed Bridget's face as she blurted out, "Call me gobsmacked! You went into a pub to drink a pint with the colonel? Whatever possessed you to make such a request let alone for him to honour it?"

"I felt certain I would find him a willing accomplice for such a simple and rather innocent request although he had no idea what he bargained for. I became so caught up in the lively spirit of the place and all the spontaneous performances, I stood up and recited St. Brigid's Blessing in the native Irish language."

"Saints preserve us, you did not! I am doubly gobsmacked. Reciting that old Irish blessing in the forbidden language in such a public place! If your mam or your brother hear of it they'll lock you up in a convent to be sure. Oh la, how I would loved to have been there to see you; it must have been a sight to behold."

"Oh, Birdie, it was exhilerating. No matter what comes of it, I will always treasure the excitement of this day. To be always trapped in such a confining society when there is so much more to be seen of the world. If I am found out, I shall pay any penance that is required for the delight of enjoying the music, the singing, the poetry, the ribald jokes, the camaraderie; if it is my undoing it will have been worth it."

Bridget and Catherine had been friends since they were girls and Bridget, who was four years older, had been tasked with watching over the restless and curious Catherine when her governess needed help or when wandering in the gardens was at hand. She was a robust girl, plump, cheerful, with red hair, freckles, and a ready smile. In private Catherine always used the nickname Birdie, a habit formed as a toddler who struggled to pronounce 'Bridget' and it became a joke between them since both liked the name, and laughed at the implication that Birdie was always on a perch listening. Birdie's mother had been the assistant cook at the Dalrymple estate, and when the viscount passed away and the dowager and her daughter moved to a smaller nearby estate, she was assigned to be head cook and her daughter became the personal maid to Catherine, after much lobbying on the part of her young mistress. Their solidarity was built around adventurousness, trust, and the secret forbidden language they shared.

"Oh Miss, do you think you will be caught out?" asked Birdie. "Gossip has a way of spreading swiftly and it seems you were hardly discreet. Having a pint in a public place tis one thing, but making a spectacle of yourself tis sure to set local tongues wagging and you were dressed too finely to go unnoticed in a pub, for the gentry will always stand out.

"And what did your colonel make of all this? Was it in your plans to discourage any thoughts of courtship he had by exhibiting yourself in such a way? If your mam finds out he conspired in this public transgression, she may never let him cross your threshold again. Tis very sly of you to discourage a suitor by entrapping him in a plot your mam would forbid, as well as cause him to reconsider his interest in you based on his better judgement. Killing two birds with one stone is clever indeed, Miss."

"He begins his journey to the south and west in a few days but plans to call tomorrow before he departs so we shall see if my eccentricity has discouraged him thoroughly enough. As for Mamma, if I am exposed I shall deny all, knowing that never again will she allow me to go anywhere without supervision including Trinity College to meet with dear old Dean Fitzgerald. Sometimes great reward requires great risk and I shall never regret this day so long as I live and you, Birdie, must pledge to keep my secret, for I depend on your discretion more than anything."

* ~ * ~ * ~ *

Colonel Fitzwilliam arrived as promised the next day and greeted Catherine with a bow and a conspiritorial smile when first she entered the drawing room where he had been chatting with her mother.

"Catherine, my dear," said her mother, "Colonel Fitzwilliam has just been sharing his delight at the private viewing of those ancient books you so treasure and remarking on his enjoyment in meeting Dean Fitzgerald. Such an amiable man and a very close friend of your father's for so many years. I am afraid your precocity with languages attracted the attention of many of your father's colleagues, but Dean Fitzgerald has been a consistently dependable friend to you and helped foster your interest in antiquities, which I cannot quite fathom but have reconciled myself to accept. If only you took as much interest in your social obligations and planning for your own future happiness, instead of locking yourself away in your study translating Lord knows what. Women were never intended to be scholars as I told your father repeatedly.

"Do forgive me, Colonel, for I have no wish to importune you with these small family disputes that every so often occur; I am sure you understand my concerns for my daughter's well being and happiness."

"I do, indeed. So it is true in many families," he replied. "I wonder if I could prevail on Miss Carteret to take a turn about the garden on such a lovely afternoon? I depart soon on my journey and would enjoy seeing the local prospects as a point of comparison to the new countryside I shall encounter."

"Ah, yes, you are about to embark on your travels to the south and the wilderness of the western coast; pray take care to avoid pirates, Colonel, and angry Papist peasants with no love for the English who are as numerous as rabbits, lack restraint in their habits, and engage in pugilism at every opportunity. A turn in the garden is just the thing for it is such a delightful, balmy day and I am sure my daughter will be very pleased to walk with you, is it not so my dear?"

Eager to exit before her mother continued her diatribe, Catherine led the way to the garden, exasperated by the tone of the conversation and anxious to blunt its impact. They walked silently for a few moments while she tried to gather her thoughts.

"Take heart, Miss Carteret. It can be safely stated that an eligible person of marriageable age is frequently subjected to the ignominy of being singled out by those members of their family determined to see them attached; though the pressures may be different for your sex than mine, the weight of the burden is shared by both."

"There is no hiding from the truth of which you speak and I so abhor subterfuge," replied Catherine. "The relentless pursuit by my mother to secure a match for me is equalled only by my persistent rejection of the notion of marrying at all; I object to the idea of becoming the property of a husband, and embrace my ability to pursue my interests at will, thanks to a financial bequest from my father which supports my independence, much to the dismay of my mother, and the ruin of her dearest aspirations."

"We are, all of us born into society, subject to the forces of family expectations based on dated notions of marriage as a financial contract designed to build family wealth and the prospect of inheritance for future generations. Like you, as a second son not in line to inherit, I experience similar family pressures to marry from my family. You are blessed to have a protected inheritance to ensure your independence while I am expected to choose a wife based on the potential size of her dowry. Fortunately, I too have managed to accumulate enough wealth to protect my independence, much to the vexation of my father.

"I was relieved from one of those pressures with the marriage of my cousin, Georgianna, to Dr. Baldwin, as my father had no reservations about pressing me to marry that young lady of whom I had been a joint guardian along with my cousin, Darcy, since she was a child. The prospect of such a connection between myself and a young lady who looked upon me as a brother was unthinkable, even though she likely would have been compliant, should Darcy have wished it and I been amenable. With that possibilty eliminated, my father now intends for me to marry another cousin originally intended for Darcy, which was the dearest wish of his mother and her sister, but that plan was thwarted when Darcy fell in love and secured the affections of his wife, Elizabeth.

"To marry without love, to me, is an abomination, but to marry to satisfy family expectations concerned only with expanding wealth and social standing is insupportable. We live in an age where natural affection must be given some consideration, unlike in the past, when it was treated as a transactional business arrangement."

"We are, both of us, independent minded it seems, although as a woman I am subjected to more constraints," replied Catherine. "You are able to live independently and seek adventure where you will while I have the misfortune of having to conceal my knowledge and interests as best I can, in order to adhere to society's expectations and limitations."

"If I may be so bold to point out, you seem to have defied some of those limitations already, most recently at the Gerty Browne pub," he laughed. "I must say your recitation captivated the entire audience including myself, many of whom were both astonished and moved listening to you; hence, I wonder if it was your plan from the outset to engage me in a scheme to breach propriety by visiting a local pub and performing, or a spontaneous reaction to the atmosphere and ebullience of the crowd? Did you mean to dissuade me from forming any future plans of accompanying you to a public place, by shocking me with your request and the unrehearsed display of your multiple talents? You may have meant to discourage me but alas, I found it quite charming."

Catherine could not withhold the slightest of smiles when she responded, "My mother certainly would not find it charming and my entire family would be appalled if they heard of it. I do hope I can depend on your discretion."

"Always," he replied. "I wonder if you, in turn, will honour a request? I leave on my expedition tomorrow and wish to send you correspondence while I'm away. Since you are at least partially the inadvertent instigator of this voyage, and tethered by the constraints society imposes on you, it would please me to share news of this adventure as it transpires. If you agree, I shall, of course, ask permission of your mother, as a letter to you would not escape her notice and I do not wish to raise her ire."

The sudden agitation of spirit Catherine felt at this request was bewildering in ways she was not used to experiencing. While she enjoyed Colonel Fitzwilliam's company, his intelligence, his wit, his curiosity, the ease with which he navigated society so unlike herself; she felt suddenly cautious about sending the wrong signals that might encourage him to believe there was an attachment possible. To be sure he was a desirable match for someone of her rank if she was amenable, but amenable she was not. The question was whether she could continue to enjoy his attentions and companionship without offering encouragement of anything beyond platonic friendship. She was relieved he was going away and she could settle back into her self-contained life; she was undeniably interested in learning about his travels, but what would agreeing to receive correspondence mean? To her family it would be cause for celebration, but would it encourage expectations on his part to which she could never accede? It was a connundrum.

"I have no doubt Mamma will embrace such a request and I have no objection to it, but allow me to admonish you that artifice of any kind is abhorrent to me, and should I accept your most generous offer, I would not wish to have my interest in your travels be misconstrued as anything of a more personal nature."

"You have been exceedingly clear on that point since first we met in Bath," he said with a smile and nod. "My only wish is to satisfy your abundantly curious nature with the intelligence I gather along the way, and to share more of the details when I return to Dublin in a few weeks. You may rest assured, I have no greater expectations than the pleasure of relaying my experience on this quest to someone who will appreciate the details and the historical relevance." They continued to walk the grounds and climbed a hill for a better prospect before returning to the house where he bid farewell to her and the Dowager Viscountess Dalrymple.

"Catherine, my dear, you have restored my faith in your better judgement at last. Colonel Fitzwilliam wishes to correspond with you while he is away. What a feather in your cap! I believe he has developed feelings for you and I must admonish you, do not dissuade his interest. Be open to having a change of heart and let yours be stirred by the attentions of such a fine gentleman."

"I assure you, Mamma, my intentions regarding my future remain unchanged; it is at your own hazard to allow yourself to think otherwise. I have an interest in Colonel Fitzwilliam's destination and what he discovers, no more than that."

"You may speak for yourself but not for him so do not underestimate his interests."

Chapter 5

"What news!" announced the dowager viscountess to Catherine and her daughter-in-law, Augusta, at afternoon tea as she waved a letter that had just been delivered. "I have just received this from our cousin, Lady Elizabeth Bertram, announcing she and Sir Thomas plan a visit to Ireland as part of the celebration of their recent marriage. She says they wish to visit us as well as journey north to Ulster in search of linen and to see a gifted lacemaker with whom she is acquainted. You must remember the beautiful lace she wore on her wedding day, Catherine, I am sure I've never seen any so fine. They hope to stay with us for a few weeks and of course visit with you and Charles as well, Augusta."

"How sublime, but really, dear Mamma, do you not think it best for them to be guests at Rathclare Hall? Afterall, Elizabeth is married to a baronet now and deserves the highest consideration under these new circumstances. I am sure it was no trouble for you to host her during her time of bereavement when she was still a single woman, and, of course, it was so thoughtful and generous of you to take her under your wing, but now that she is married, it seems only fitting that they should stay with us. It will be a delight to renew her acquaintance with our friends and introduce her husband into Dublin society now that she has married so successfully. Charles and I will send an invitation right away if you agree; how charming it will be to present them, and she is such a lovely woman, so elegant with such refined tastes. It will take the burden off of you to entertain them and it will be ever so much more pleasant for them, do you not agree? We do want to make a good impression on Sir Thomas."

"You are quite right, Augusta, your estate has far more suitable accomodations with many more amusements for them; I am sure they will welcome an invitation from you and Charles."

"We must have a ball while they are here. What a delightful idea! Once the dates are settled I will formulate a plan for putting up white soup. Dearest Catherine, when is your colonel expected back in Dublin? I understand he will be writing to you while he is away so, of course, you must keep us informed of his schedule so that he can attend the ball. What an agreeable man he is and how lovely that he has come all this way to see you; a triumph really. We must include him in the scheme for, if memory serves, he was a witness to the marriage on behalf of Sir Thomas. Such felicity to bring them together again, do you not agree?" she asked followed by an expressive smile.

"Augusta, let me be perfectly clear that the gentleman of whom you speak is not 'my colonel' and the anticipated correnspondence has no significance beyond his offer to share such history as he uncovers during his travels, since I was the source of intellience about the subject. A 'triumph' it is not and I beseech you to temper your comments along with your imagination," stated Catherine with some indignation.

While importuned by the inference of her 'triumph' with Colonel Fitzwilliam and the perception of an attachment between them, Catherine was relieved by the change of venue decided on for the Bertrams, and amused by the eagerness of Augusta to host them due to her cousin's improved social standing. Were Elizabeth still a single woman with modest resources, dependent on relatives and friends for her accomodations, the invitation to stay at Rathclare Hall would not likely have been issued.

In view of the imposition experienced during her last visit, the prospect of her cousin returning with her new husband, Sir Thomas, was odious for she found them both to be insipid. During the months that Elizabeth Elliot had been with them, Catherine found her cousin repellent with her vanities, airs, and vacuous conversation; resented her intrusions into daily life; and was appalled by the sheer arrogance of her suggestions for Catherine to change her style of attire in order to improve her appearance, as though her cousin was the sole arbiter of good taste and fashion, and, even worse, under the assumption that Catherine had any concern about such matters. The plain manner in which she chose to dress and the amount of time she spent in her study was by choice, calculated to serve her own desires, and required no guidance from this invasive cousin whose comments were offensive. unwarranted, and unwelcomed. To make matters worse was the general presumption by her family that courtship was afoot despite all protestations to the contrary.

* ~ * ~ * ~ *

It was with great relief she stepped into the carriage for her scheduled visit to Dean Fitzgerald at Trinity College and she looked forward to a reprieve from the scrutiny and vexatious insinuations that were so diverting to her family. Despite her mother's pleadings, she travelled alone with the parchments and manuscripts she'd been studying on ancient Rome. Immersing herself in examinations of the cultural and political life of its founders was always engrossing; just the thing to take her mind off the current state of affairs in her own life with the pending arrival of Sir Thomas and his wife, which was an irritant, as well as the return of Colonel Fitzwilliam, which she reluctantly acknowledged both enticed and exasperated her. The upheaval to her peace of mind was irksome; she was eager to hear of his exploits but reluctant to have him intrude on her family life and upset the delicate detente she had established with her family about her determination to remain a single woman.

The greeting by Dean Fitzgerald did nothing to appease her perturbation as his civilities centred on his approbation of the distinguished visitor who had accompanied her to view the *Book of Kells*. "Such a man of consequence with a most pleasing address, well informed, and affable," enthused the dean. "I was quite taken with him and his obvious admiration of you, my dear Catherine. Well done indeed!"

Her exasperation at having to listen to yet another person of her acquaintaince praise her good fortune at being the object of attention by such a dignified gentleman, such an exemplary example of well-bred manhood, was almost more than she could tolerate gracefully. Her patience having nearly reached its limit, she persevered to change the subject as quickly as possible to the topics of mutual interest that they were meant to discuss. His pursuit of the subject and efforts to congratulate her were gradually diverted to more meaningful discourse.

As they looked over an ancient map of Rome and applied her academic study of the various public buildings and temples to those on the map, Dean Fitzgerald announced that a former tutor of Catherine's, who had been living in Rome with a stipend from the College, would be arriving in Dublin soon. "Surely you remember Mr. Duncan Woulff; as a young man he tutored you and your brother for almost two years starting when you were but a girl of perhaps 2 and 10, until we arranged for him to take up ancient studies in Rome on behalf of the College, where he has been for over a decade. I am certain he will be delighted to make your acquaintance again; he always spoke highly of you as his most proficient student, so very adroit with languages and conversant in so many at such a young age; in truth, we all were amazed at your abilities including your dear father."

Catherine remembered Mr. Woulff vividly as perhaps the first and only infatuation she had ever experienced in her youth. He was a young man of twenty, a student at Trinity who had been recommended by Dean Fitzgerald as a Latin tutor. Charles had neither the aptitude nor interest to take Latin studies seriously, certainly not with the same zeal he had for sport, but Catherine was a clever student already, well versed in the language, which earned his favour and attention instantly. He was tall with unusual hazel eyes, a combination of light brown and green, a kindly smile, and a courtly manner; as quick with praise as she was eager for it, and providing a mantle of approbation that was both reassuring and encouraging; a welcome respite from the constant reproaches from her mother about the time she spent on her studies. She basked under the glow of his praise and blossomed under his tutelage. He was conversant in French, Spanish, and Italian, having travelled in his youth, which allowed them to expand their exchanges to broader topics of geography and history. Her father's study had ancient maps mounted on the wall which they would study together and he would present intriguing games to test both her knowledge and language skills. She felt accepted, understood, and appreciated and was forlorn when he abruptly left to take a new position at a university in Rome, especially because she never had a chance to say goodbye to him. The prospect of meeting him again was welcome news.

Chapter 6

When Sir Thomas Bertram arrived with his new bride, Lady Elizabeth Bertram, the level of their social engagements increased markedly, much to Catherine's perturbation and her mother's delight; the dowager viscountess was eager for opportunities to display her attachment to the lovely cousin, whom she had rather relunctantly taken under her wing while grieving the loss of her father, Sir Walter Elliot. Even though the Carteret and Bertram families had been estranged and only recently reconciled in Bath, Sir Walter and his eldest daughter, Elizabeth, had attached themselves so vigorously to the dowager viscountess at every opportunity for exposure in society, that they managed to quickly ingratiate themselves, and when the following year, Sir Walter was felled by a series of strokes, the dowager felt it a duty to invite Elizabeth to stay with them in Ireland during her mourning period.

The outrage committed by Sir Walter's heir, Sir William Elliot, in slighting Miss Elliot by significantly foreshortening the amount of her inheritance due to the level of debt of the family estate, meant her reduced circumstances forced an unwelcome, immediate dependence on family and friends. Since Elizabeth was still a notable beauty and the only unmarried daughter of Sir Walter, her situation as a single woman past the age of thirty with expensive tastes and an inflated sense of superiority, meant introducing her to Dublin society in hopes of finding a potential suitor and seemed a better plan than relying on her married sisters to host her in their homes, an unthinkable outcome for all concerned. Now here she was returned, having made a conquest of her own, married to a baronet like her father, but this time she had acquired the title she so ardently longed for, 'Lady Bertram'. The current Viscountess Dalrymple and the dowager Viscountess Dalrymple could not have been more delighted to welcome the newlyweds and plan such lively entertainments to satisfy them all, save for Catherine.

The first order of business was a reception at Rathclare Hall for the pillars of society to meet the happy couple; the occasion saw Lady Bertram relishing the newfound approbation that her elevated status as the wife of a baronet afforded her. As a single lady mourning the loss of her father during her last visit, her social engagements were necessarily limited by the sad event and, while pitiable, although still a very handsome woman, her status as a spinster was not matched by a sizeable inheritance to enhance her physical attractions. On the arm of her husband, she was now obligingly sought after and admired as a superior addition to the noble family connections of her cousins in Dublin.

Among the guests at the reception was Mrs. Margaret Jameson, niece of the dowager Viscountess who helped raise her after her mother died. She and Catherine were never close while growing up and Margaret left home at an early age to marry a wealthy businessman and estate owner, Magnus Jameson. When her husband fell ill a few years after their marriage and passed away, he left her a substantial inheritance and a young daughter, Mary, who was now sixteen years of age, tall, fair, full formed, and high spirited with a mother who doted on her.

A splendid supper was served and Catherine found herself seated near her cousin Margaret and Miss Mary Jameson. "I understand that you have had a gentleman caller visit from England, the son of an earl no less," began Margaret. "Aunt Caroline and Augusta spoke rapturously of him; a fine looking gentleman, dignified, charming, and eligible. I was told he is travelling to our western shores but will return soon and I do so look forward to making his acquaintance; surely he will be in attendance at the ball Augusta is planning for Sir Thomas and Lady Bertram."

"I am sure I would very much like to meet the gentleman as well," chimed in Mary. "I would like to hear about his adventures on the high seas. Mamma and I will be on an adventure ourselves soon. She has agreed to take me on a grand tour of Europe and we plan to spend an extended period in Italy. I do so long to see Rome and ride gondolas in Venice. What greater felicity can there be than travelling to exotic places? Have you been to Italy, Catherine? I understand you speak Italian ever so well. Have you any books you could lend me so that I might begin to learn the language? I would be ever so grateful. Do you not agree that it is far more pleasurable to travel in a country when you know the language?"

Catherine hardly had time to pivot from the presumptuous comments of Margaret to the stream of questions from Mary. She decided to ignore the vexing comments of the first and focus on answering the questions of the second. "How stimulating a European tour with your mother will be and I applaud you for your desire to learn a language. As it happens, I am fluent in many languages including Italian and I am sure I can spare an Italian dictionary for you to begin your studies. Mind you, it will require you to learn vocabulary as well as how to parse verbs. I have never had the opportunity to visit Italy but I have studied its ancient history and am conversant in Latin which is at the core of all the Romance languages. If you apply yourself to learn one you will be able to learn others as well, with the key requirement being that you must apply yourself and study."

"How thrilling to learn a Romance language, don't you agree, Mamma? We must call soon at Rathclare Park so I can begin my studies with Catherine," to which Catherine replied, "I shall loan you books but you will have to begin your studies on your own unless your mother wishes to consider hiring a tutor to help you learn."

Turning to Margaret she said, "As to our acquaintance with Colonel Fitzwilliam whom we met in Bath, he did make a courtesy call on us when he arrived in Dublin and was kind enough to join us one afternoon at my brother's estate, but I have no expectation that his travels will allow him to accomodate an invitation to a ball and I would never be so presumptuous to assume it, nor should anyone else."

* ~ * ~ * ~ *

Shortly after her arrival, Lady Bertram and Augusta called at Rathclare Park while Sir Thomas was engaged in a shooting match with the viscount. Catherine was called from her study to join them in the drawing room by her mother.

"How well you look, Cousin Catherine," said Elizabeth. "The green becomes you so much more than the drab greys and browns that you are usually partial to. Ah, such felicity to be here once again; I am reminded of the many delightful evenings we sat in this very room admiring the view of the garden. I will always be grateful for your kindness during that melancholy time in my life following the death of my dear father, so unmoored by the loss, and the selfish deceit of his heir."

"Say no more of that trying time, my dear, your fortunes have risen far beyond anything you could have dreamed back when you were overwhelmed with deep sorrow; consider only the felicity of your current situation now that you are happily married. Do tell us more about your new home and family. Does Mansfield Park measure up to your elevated tastes cultivated under your dear father's guidance? And what of his family? How do you find his children? Have you formed an attachment to any of them? Have they embraced you properly as a stepmother with all the respect due you as the new lady of the house? Pray tell us how you fare in your new home?" queried Lady Dalrymple.

"The estate itself is quite beautiful with a park five miles round, a spacious modern-built house well placed and well screened although in want of new furnishings; the baronetcy of Sir Thomas lacks the history of my father's which had the dignity of having been established under Charles II, and is not new made as so many have been in the last century, including my husband's, who was a member of Parliament you know. As to the family they are agreeable save for the eldest son who had a propensity for gaming and incurring debts that were a drain on the fortunes of the estate. Sir Thomas did what he could to manage his son's excesses but I am especially grateful that the wedding gift from my husband, newly acquired property in Antigua, was kept separate from the inheritance of his heir, who, by all appearances, is chastened after surviving a severe illness. He caused great injury to his younger brother, having robbed Edmund of more than half the income that ought to have been his in a perferment, in order for the elder brother's debts to be dispatched. I pray my dear husband lives a long and healthy life so he can ensure his namesake does not fall into bad habits again and cost the family their entire inheritance. Edmund, the younger son is a more docile and agreeable man. He took orders and married his cousin, Fanny, who was taken in by the family at the age of nine; a vapid, compliant creature with no taste, little conversation, but blessed with a pretty face. They live nearby and are of no consequence save to attend family gatherings.

"As to the daughters, now there is a story to be told, one of which I was aware prior to our marriage. One would think that well bred, attractive young ladies raised in such an impeccable environment would have offered no trouble to their father but such was not the case. The oldest daughter, Maria, had the good fortune to make an alliance that was unquestionably advantageous, a connection of just the right sort, to a Mr. Rushworth whose income was larger than that of her father with a fine estate and a house in town; although he was said to be a rather dull and unimposing young man. During the engagement and against all rationality, she became enamored with a wealthy young man who was visitng in town with his sister, whom the Bertram family had taken up acquaintance. His sister, Mary Crawford, was a pretty, vivacious creature while Henry, although dark and plain, had such a pleasing address that his countenance soon made him attractive to both the Bertram sisters. The Crawfords each had an inheritance that made them very eligible prospects, and a mutual attraction began to form between Mary and Edmund Bertram, while Maria, the recipient of the romantic attentions of Henry, interpreted them as his wish for a more permanent connection, and would have thrown off her engagement had he asked. Instead, he removed himself to London and a disappointed Maria proceeded with her marriage to Mr. Rushworth, and enjoyed all the benefits that his wealth and situation could provide as a leading socialite in London.

"Later, when Henry returned, he developed an infatuation with Fanny and began a courtship that she quite foolishly rejected; such capriciousness on either side begs the question of sound judgement considering her station in life as well as his; for surely there were more eligible young ladies available to a man of his rank including Julia Bertram, the younger sister. Fanny seems a very odd choice for Henry to have pursued considering her want of those advantageous female attributes most likely to lure a young man of good fortune, although she did eventually succeed in attracting Edmund with her charms, which still remains a mystery to me."

"Such a deliciously convoluted story," declared Augusta. "Surely the newly married Mrs. Rushworth must have enjoyed her elevated status in society even if she was enamored with another, felt slighted by his behaviour, and disappointed in love. One learns to recover from such distractions. And her younger sister, is she still a single woman or has she married?"

"Oh, yes indeed, Julia married, but to the exasperation of my dear husband, she eloped with a gentleman friend of her brother, Thomas, much to his disappointment. Worse yet, Maria rekindled her relationship with Henry when they met again in London, abandoned all reason along with her husband, and ran off with her paramour. I'm sure she was piqued by the news of his offer of marriage to her cousin, Fanny, and determined to remind him of the many charms that he had overlooked in herself. Of course, she was immediately divorced by her husband and now lives in isolation under the guardianship of her aunt, Mrs. Norris, with the kindly support of Sir Thomas. He has since reconciled with Julia and her husband as well, and we dine with them occasionally."

"Divorced? What a stain on the family's reputation," commented the dowager viscountess. "It is well that Sir Thomas was forthcoming with this information prior to your agreement to marry; afterall, we must accept the bad with the good in life, and being so comfortably settled in your rightful station in society is to your credit, no matter the behaviour of your new stepdaughters."

"Thank you for your understanding, dearest cousin. The pity is that Maria is such a lovely creature, poised, charming, witty, all of those traits you look for in a fashionable woman. More's the pity she threw away her elevated station in life for a passing flirtation that damaged her reputation irretrievably but had no ill affect on his whatsoever. If her husband hadn't been so dull-witted she might have held on or, done the sensible thing and had a surreptitious affair, instead of ruining her life by running off with a rogue. I do wish there was a way to somehow redeem her reputation so she could rejoin social circles and find enjoyment in life again rather than wasting away with her shrewish aunt. Of all the children, I enjoy her company the most and find it such a waste of feminine pulchritude and elegant manners but, for now, there is nothing to be done. Her dowry remains with her former husband and she depends on the kindness of her father for all of her needs. Love affairs can be a dangerous pastime."

"Such iniquity is difficult to dismiss even if one feels sympathy; a woman's reputation must be above reproach," said the dowager viscountess.

"Is there nothing to be done?" asked Augusta. "Perhaps there are some in Dublin society who would more obligingly overlook such a transgression for a truly exceptional woman of fashion who is able to charm and amuse. We must take it under advisement for now."

The abhorrence Catherine felt at this discussion was matched only by her observation that this was a fitting commentary on married life for a woman. Marriage was an obligation even if it required marrying a fool so long as he enjoyed wealth and social status. It is a business arrangement regardless of emotional attachment, and the delights of an amorous attraction should be enjoyed in secret or foresworn altogether. Break the rules of society and the punishment falls solely on the woman including the loss of inheritance, property, and children if there are any; all belongs to the husband.

Chapter 7

Catherine was relieved when the visitors departed and her mother retired, especially so because a letter arrived addressed to her from Colonel Fitzwilliam. Had they been present, the invasion of her privacy would have been inevitable. As it was, she knew her mother would insist on having the letter read aloud but for the moment it was her's alone.

Dear Miss Carteret,

I am in your debt, Madam, for provoking the impulse to travel the coast of your fair country by sea in pursuit of treasures that can never be plundered, save by the gathering of anecdotes to be chronicled and shared, for that is my purpose in writing of the first leg of my journey. If you have never had the chance to visit, you would be pleased with Waterford situated on three sides by water and marshes with only the west side having required fortifications. I like to think of Vikings landing here, pillaging at first but then settling down to establish communities in the 9th century. It was Henry II who landed here and first claimed to be Lord of Ireland formally establishing an English foothold, while many years later, Henry VII gave it a motto: "Waterford remains the untaken city", based I suppose on its fortifications. The Waterford crystal factory was as notable for the beauty of its products as the intricate craftsmanship that goes into creating them. George and William Penrose founded the factory in 1783 using a new process that included flint glass which contributes to the brilliancy of the crystal, and the heat from the firing furnaces is daunting; how the craftsmen tolerate it is a wonderment, but I know you would be fascinated by the process for whatever amount of time you could bear it. We journey thither to Connacht tomorrow to avoid risk of death at the hands of the Dearg Dur, a female vampire known to prey on single men. Be not alarmed for my safety, I assure you that I never move about alone after nightfall. I wonder if you've ever heard of this legendary figure known to the locals of Waterford? It would give me great pleasure to be the first to introduce you to a piece of Waterford history that may have escaped your notice, the existence of which may not have reached the scholarly heights of Trinity College. Dearg Dur was said to be an astounding beauty who was pressed into an unwanted marriage by her father to a wealthy clan Chieftain in exchange for riches and extensive property. It was said she wore red and gold on her wedding day and sat alone mourning the loss of her avowed true love, a local farmer to whom she had pledged her troth. That very day she vowed vengence on her father for his betrayal and she was locked away by her abusive husband as a trophy for himself alone. Despondent and abandoned, she refused all sustainance allowing herself to waste away until her life was gone. While her family enjoyed newfound riches and her husband immediately found a new wife, her lost love visited her grave daily and mourned for her. Compelled by her vow of vengeance on her father and consumed by anger still, on the anniversary of her death she climbed from her coffin, returned to her family home where her father slept and touched her lips to his, sucking the very life out of him. Still unsated, she visited her callous husband who was surrounded by women and fulfilling his lusty desires, unaware of her presence. In her rage she sent the women screaming from the room and set upon him drawing every breath from his lungs and every drop of blood from his body. Filled with bloodlust forever more, the corpse bride used her beauty to prey on young men and lured them to their death, sinking her teeth into their exposed necks to drink their blood and relieve her unquenchable thirst. I imperiled my life by visiting Strongbow's Tree where the remains of Dearg Dur are buried with rocks covering her grave to prevent her from wandering, although sometimes the rocks are displaced and she wanders still. However, I chose to be cautious and visited midday rather than at night, but lest my visit have disturbed her, I make my escape in the morning and have a guard posted at my door this very evening with hopes that if she is filled with bloodlust, she'll choose the guard over myself, as I don't wish to tempt fate and miss my journey to visit the

home of the Pirate Queen of Connacht. I trust I have your
support in this matter.

   I remain your humble servant,
   Colonel Edward Fitzwilliam

Catherine's surprise at this most unconventional letter was exceeded only by her amusement at its contents for she could barely contain her laughter not to mention her admiration for the author conveying a story she had not heard before. Perhaps it would have been more entertaining if the recently departed guests, Augusta and Lady Bertram, along with her mother, had been exposed to the story; she could imagine the horrified look on their faces and the mirth she would surely have enjoyed witnessing it. It was the most entertaining letter she had ever received, the contents were completely unexpected, and the writer had captivated her interest such that, despite her misgivings, she was eager to receive his next correspondence.

Her mother, having learned that a letter arrived, was impatient to know the contents but Catherine was able to temporarily demure reading it aloud, stating merely that he wrote of the layout of Waterford and the city's history as well as about the crystal factory, and of a local legend he described that was dismissed as hardly worth mentioning. Not to be dissuaded, when Augusta, Lady Bertram, Mrs. Jameson and her daughter, Mary came to call a few days later, they conspired to demand the letter be read in full and included all the usual innuendos of the remarkable conquest Catherine had made by way of receiving private correspondence from the son of an earl who had, most obligingly, sought the approval of her mother to write.

Despite her vexation at their inferences, Catherine could barely maintain her composure and keep from smiling as she read the missive to her audience and watched their attention shift from polite admiration to rapt attention followed by shock as the story unveiled.

"Oh, it is just like reading *The Mysteries of Udolpho*, I have shivers down my spine!" exclaimed Mary. "Do you imagine Colonel Fitzwilliam was truly afraid of being attacked by a beautiful vampire? It is ever so exciting and now he ventures even further in search of a pirate queen. What could be more thrilling?"

"Mary, dear, you have been reading far too many novels; pray exert yourself and endeavour to contain your overactive imagination," declared the dowager. "Colonel Fitzwilliam could not have intended to alarm us with his letter for he must understand we are all rational creatures and not easily subjected to fright; clearly he meant to entertain his reader."

The conversation continued as the women murmured amongst themselves and postulated about the colonel's plans and intentions until finally moving on to other subjects including the pending tour of Europe to introduce Mary to a broader cultural experience. Mary again broached the topic about her desire to learn Italian giving Catherine an excuse to retreat to her study in search of books that would help Mary learn the language; a brief but welcome reprieve from the casual references to courtship and rank bandied about in the drawing room. When she reentered the room she was relieved to hear the subject of conversation had pivoted again.

"We leave for Ulster on Monday and I am so looking

forward to selecting new linens in Belfast; we have visited the Linen Hall in Dublin but the selection is not nearly so extensive or exclusive as those to be found in Belfast and we are in such need of new fabrics at Mansfield Park. I'm quite taken with a particular lacemaker in the area as well, who creates the most exquisite designs you can possibly imagine, ever so intricate. I shall not be content until I've previewed all of her work and made my selections or perhaps commissioned new ones. Dear Sir Thomas is ever so indulgent; he admires elegance and sophistication as much as I do. His first wife was a rather retiring woman who preferred to stay at home with her pugs and collect fine cashmere shawls from the East Indies as a sign of her prosperity. Now that he has a young, energetic, fashionable wife, he takes great pride in showcasing me and spending more time in town; afterall one cannot always be limited to life on a great estate alone. This will be his first trip to Ulster and we plan to explore Armagh as well as Belfast; he says nothing will please him more than an extended wedding trip with his bride. Marriage has turned out to be a much more enriching experience than I ever could have imagined," extolled Elizabeth. "You really should consider it yourself, Cousin Catherine."

"Importune me no longer with your vanities and advice!" was the first thought to cross Catherine's mind but she contained the impulse and instead demurely responded that she was still commited to a single life and had no desire or need to marry. As the group departed, Mary thanked Catherine for loaning her the books and asked if she could visit again soon to practice what she learned in conversation. "You must exert yourself to learn the vocabulary and practice the sentence structure if we are to converse the next time you visit," replied Catherine. She had little confidence Mary would put forth the effort but at least had to give her credit for challenging herself to improve her mind and expand her horizons, although she had no intention of becoming a tutor to the young lady.

Chapter 8

The Bertrams were off to Ulster much to Catherine's relief as it meant a respite from all the social functions centred around their stay at Rathclare Hall and the demands on her time. She was finally able to focus on a request from Dean Fitzgerald to translate some ancient Roman scrolls and looked forward to a trip to Trinity College to see her old friend. She valued the relationship with the elderly gentleman and the opportunity to exchange ideas; a reminder of the support and nurturing of her unique gifts that she had received from her father. How fortunate she had been that he gave her space to discover her natural talents rather than suppressing them as her mother had done. Visits to Trinity were the highlight of her existence and she depended on the occasions to validate her life choices; there she was treated as an intellectual and scholar even though, as a woman, she was not allowed to attend classes or claim a profession. She treasured those moments in time, when she was temporarily released from her gender role and treated as an equal. She even enjoyed the informality of his calling her by her first name as he had since she was a child.

When she reached the dean's office he greeted her effusively. "My dear Catherine, I have such a surprise for you. Come and sit, I'll return in just a moment and will add such felicity to your day. Tempus fugit." He quickly returned with a tall, imposing gentleman of about five and thirty with a pleasing address, a striking countenance, and more finely attired than the usual collection of scholars and professors that inhabited the halls of Trinity.

"Buon giorno, Signora Carteret," he said with a courtly bow. Do you remember me for I shall never forget you."

Dean Fitzgerald chortled in the background. "Have you forgotten your former tutor, Duncan Woulff? He tells me you were the finest student he ever had the pleasure of teaching."

A flood of memories surged in Catherine's mind as she sorted out the features of the man standing before her and his resemblence to the handsome tutor from her youth. She had been about twelve and her brother ten years old when her father hired him, and contrived to get the approval of her mother to allow her to attend morning classes. His countenance was fuller now as was his well-made frame, his hair was still light brown and his hazel eyes a mix of golden brown with a hint of green, his complexion was tan indicating time spent in the sun and there were fine lines around his eyes indicative of an amiable nature. Most of all she recognised the deep dimple in his chin and the warm smile.

A lively conversation transpired as they recalled the two

years he spent with her family teaching her brother to conjugate Latin verbs while challenging her linguistic abilities in Latin, Greek, French, Spanish, and Italian. He had been a student at Trinity when introduced to her father, but had travelled extensively with his family as his father had been a trade consultant to various European governments. His departure from the family had been abrupt and she had missed his presence; none of her other tutors had been quite as engaging, good-natured, and agreeable. His replacements had all been humourless, restrictive, and demanding even though she always came prepared for class and never missed assignments.

"I trust your brother, the viscount, is in good health. I suspect his memories of studying under my tutelage are not nearly so gratifying as his memories of his exploits hunting, fencing, and riding; he was always an enthusiastic sportsman and a reluctant student, unlike you, Miss Carteret. Dean Fitzgerald speaks the truth, you were always and still remain the most preeminent scholar of my acquaintance. You challenged me as much as I challenged you and it was exhilarating to intellectually spar with you; indeed, it was a privilege. I was pleasantly surprised to find you are still an active scholar assisting Dean Fitzgerald rather than tucked away on an estate with a title and a brood of children. Your gifts are far too superior to be disregarded, overlooked, or underdeveloped."

"I assure you my brother is much the same as he aways was and I thank you for your kind words about my education and continued interest in linguistics and history. It has been my honour to continue to support Dean Fitzgerald's efforts to expand knowledge for students here at Trinity," replied Catherine who somehow managed to keep her composure and not blush from the praise.

The discussion shifted to the scrolls she had been studying and she was delighted to find that Mr. Woulff had much intelligence to offer to her own theories and was exceptionally well versed in the study of Roman antiquities. Having lived there for so many years, his immersion in local ancient history and locations of former temples was remarkable and she was gratified for the new points of evidence he was able to contribute to the conversation. He had carried with him some particularly valuable scrolls that the dean had been eager to acquire on behalf of the college and hoped that Catherine would be allowed to peruse. They were priceless and fragile so it was agreed that Mr. Woulff would deliver them to Rathclare Park the following week as he was also looking forward to making a courtesy call and paying his respects to her mother. It was settled that her former tutor, urbane, sophisticated, and worldly, would soon visit with the prized scrolls.

On the ride home Catherine had the opportunity to reflect on her youthful feelings towards Mr. Woulff. She realised now, at the age of seven and twenty, that he had been her first and only girlish infatuation. She had been captivated by his warm smile, kindly eyes, and reassuring manner; it was like basking in warm sunlight enjoying the glow of his approval and approbation. Although she was shy and introverted about her person, she was authoritative and challenging in her studies which he accepted and encouraged. He seemed to delight in their intellectual encounters and testing her mettle in knowledge of languages and history. She had been inconsolable when he abruptly departed and it took some time for the gloom to lift and her spirits to recover.

Age had treated him kindly. His youthful features had given way to a more chiselled countenance and muscular frame while his pleasing address and gentleman-like appearance added to his bearing. What, she wondered, would her mother have to say when Mr. Woulff came to call? Prior to the arrival of Colonel Fitzwilliam her mother might have leapt at the chance to encourage an attachment, desperate as she was to see her daughter finally married, but now his station in life would be considered entirely unsuitable in comparison to the son of an earl. Still, he was unquestionably a handsome and sophisticated man for whom social status might well be overlooked if pressed by the evidence of affection. Despite her commitment to lead a solitary life focused on scholarly pursuits, she wondered if there existed a man who could distract her from her path and whether she could overcome her mistrust of anyone who claimed to be attracted to a plain looking and socially awkward woman like herself who just happened to have a sizeable inheritance.

Chapter 9

Catherine's sister-in-law, Augusta, arrived one afternoon accompanied by Margaret and Mary Jameson who was carrying the Italian language books that Catherine had loaned her two weeks prior. Curious as to whether she had applied herself, Catherine suggested they remove themselves to her study where they could try to converse in Italian while her mother and the two ladies socialised. Her expectations were not high, since Mary struck her as a young lady with a great deal of enthusiasm but little discipline to learn a language, and who was very enamoured with the idea of travelling to far off, romantic places to display her proficiency. She was pleasantly surprised when Mary was able to respond to a few simple sentences although she struggled with pronunciation.

"You must remember, Mary, that unlike languages such as English and, especially, French, in Italian all the syllables are pronounced, none are silent," said Catherine, who then began to demonstrate the correct pronunciation. While she had little patience for teaching nor did she intend to serve that role for Mary, she did admire the young lady's efforts since she had acquired the books. "Memorising vocabulary words is the only way to develop true proficiency along with understanding sentence declension," was her advice.

"Do you think I will be capable by the time we leave for Italy?" asked Mary.

"That depends on you, Mary. Some people are blessed with an ear for languages and learn quickly, while others have to rely on repetition and practice before they succeed. Of course, the opportunity to practice conversation in the chosen language also contributes to early fluency and I shall help you when I have time available but I can not predict how quickly you will learn."

At that, a servant knocked on the door of the study and they were informed that a gentleman had arrived who was calling for Catherine. When they entered the sitting room there stood Duncan Woulff with a weathered cylindrical leather case strapped on his shoulder offering a courtly bow to the ladies before turning around to greet her with a warm smile.

"Ah, Miss Carteret, I am so pleased to find you at home. I come on assignment from Dean Fitzgerald to deliver the scrolls we discussed; they finally arrived this week along with a shipment of artifacts that I arranged to have sent from Rome ahead of my travels to Dublin. Please forgive my intrusion, I do not wish to importune you and your guests." Then, turning towards her mother, he greeted her with a courtly bow.

"Viscountess Dalrymple, what a pleasure it is to see you again. I was so sorry to hear of the loss of your husband;

please accept my sincere condolences. He was a much admired scholar and supporter of Trinity College, especially the Department of Ancient Languages and Antiquities; I greatly enjoyed getting to know him when I served as tutor to your son, Charles, and to Miss Carteret."

The ladies in the room sat in stunned silence taking in the sight of this well dressed visitor with his European airs and genteel manners, while Mary went to sit near her mother to better observe him. All were captivated by this tall, handsome stranger and sat there transfixed by him.

"Mamma, surely you remember Mr. Duncan Woulff who became our tutor when Charles turned ten years old. He was with us for almost two years before departing for Rome where he has resided these many years. I became reacquainted with him during my recent visit with Dean Fitzgerald."

"Of course, of course, I do remember Mr. Woulff. How delighted we are that you came to call and thank you for your kindly words about my dear husband. He was a gifted man indeed. May I introduce you to Charles' wife, the new Viscountess Dalrymple for I am now dowager, of course, and my niece, Mrs. Jameson, the daughter of my husband's brother, William, along with Mrs. Jameson's daughter, Mary. How extraordinary to see you after so many years, Mr. Woulff. Do tell us about your life in Rome and how you came to live there? We are all quite taken with receiving a visitor from such a distant and exotic place."

"I am still attached to Trinity, having been assigned to an affiliate in Rome as an investigator to authenticate and negotiate for ancient treasures as acquisitions on behalf of the college. I have the privilege of delivering newly discovered Roman scrolls for Miss Carteret to examine and annotate; she is a gifted researcher and linguist upon whom Dean Fitzgerald relies, an exceptional scholar of ancient Latin and Greek documents much like her father."

"I have always maintained that it is unseemly for a young woman to indulge in scholarly pursuits; too much knowledge is a misfortune she should work to conceal. However, my husband thought otherwise and supported her independence to pursue her interests and so she does. Still, we are delighted to receive you and if Catherine is the reason that brings about your visit, then we are grateful."

Augusta spoke up next. "How enchanting to make your acquaintance, Mr. Woulff and I know my husband, the viscount, would find me very deficient if I did not invite you to Rathclare Hall to renew your acquaintance with him. He would be delighted to hear about your years in Rome, I assure you; he is dotingly fond of antiquities and many examples remain at our home that were part of his father's collection. We must arrange a date straight away for you to call," she enthused with her most charming smile.

"How very obliging of you, Madam, and it would be my great pleasure to pay a visit as I have fond memories of my stay at Rathclare Hall and of my students," he replied. "Please give my compliments to your husband, the viscount."

Catherine could barely maintain her composure. How astonishing to learn that Charles was so fond of the antiquities at the residence for she recalled he had been eager to remove many of them to Rathclare Park when she and her mother moved, but Augusta had convinced him that some of the more notable pieces added a stately elegance to the home, and were a reflection of the excellence of their taste. However, she had been more than happy to send off musty maps, old books, and any goods that appeared well worn and not worthy to be shown off.

"Such felicity to meet a gentleman with extensive experience living in Rome," enthused Margaret. "My daughter and I journey thither to Italy this spring; we will be touring with a travel group but would be greatly obliged if you can provide guidance that will enhance our journey while we are in Italy. It would be so much preferable to be advised by someone knowledgable on how to engage in schemes of pleasure that we might not otherwise encounter, for I am dotingly fond of adventures off the beaten track. My daughter has already undertaken to learn the language, have you not, Mary?"

Mary, who had been openly staring at Mr. Woulff while clutching her books to her chest, blushed and from lowered eyes glanced at the comely gentleman and shyly nodded.

"Parli Italiano?" he asked.

Mary was caught off guard but Catherine came to her rescue and speaking in Italian, asserted that Miss Jameson had just begun her studies and they had this very day been practicing conversation. She then translated in English her response for the benefit of the ladies.

"Oh, indeed! Mary longs to be proficient by the time our progress begins," asserted her mother. "I am quite struck with her efforts but I worry she may not accomplish her goal without a tutor and Catherine, has not the time to dedicate to her instruction since she has occupatons of her own that absorb her, but she was most generous to lend books so my daughter could begin to learn. Mary will be staying at Rathclare Hall for a few weeks while I am away visiting cousins, and I would be greatly obliged if you would consider reviving your tutoring career even briefly on her behalf. I assure you my gratitude would be matched by generous compensation for your kindness. We all wish to see Mary's principal hopes of becoming conversant in the Italian language before we embark on our grand tour are realised, and I am certain Viscount Dalrymple and his wife will embrace the scheme."

"To be sure! We would be delighted to receive you for we are in full support of Miss Jameson's interests. You may come as often as it is convenient, for what could be more delightful than to help Mary prepare for her grand tour under your tutelage," agreed Augusta effusively.

"How splendid," responded Margaret enthusiastically, "and I look forward to having further conversations with you about the best dining establishments, exclusive places to shop and, of course, which sights to see that might not be included in our tour plan for museums and the like. How delightful it will be to have a daughter who can help us converse with the local people, it will be advantageous to be sure."

Catherine could not help but observe the unctuous behaviour of these ladies, leaning forward in their chairs, smiling coquettishly; seemingly rapturous in the presence of a courtly and charming gentleman who was clearly used to the approbation of females of all ages. Even her mother seemed enamoured as did the youngest among the ladies. She reminded herself that there was a time in her youth when she too had responded to the warm smile and kind eyes of Duncan Woulff.

At last she interceded to say, "I am sure Mr. Woulff may have more pressing obligations at the college and you must not assail him with requests he may not be free to honour."

Mr. Woulff laughed affably and replied, "How can I deny the entreaties of such a lovely group of ladies? I shall call soon at Rathclare Hall to pay my compliments to Viscount Dalrymple and we can discuss a schedule that would allow me to assist Miss Jameson in her studies without distracting me from my obligations at the college. Speaking of distractions, I wonder if we can retire to your study for a few minutes, Miss Carteret, so I can review with you these priceless scrolls I carry that I will be leaving in your capable hands? Dean Fitzgerald and I are eager for your thoughts and observations."

They stepped into her study leaving the door fully open so as not to raise questions about them being alone together and emerged a few minutes later. At that, he took his leave with a courteous bow and a promise to see them all again soon.

"Such a pleasing address," commented her mother. "So much countenance, so well made and fashionably dressed. A charming man."

"Did you notice the elegance of his boots? The finest Italian leather to be sure. Charles will be so delighted to renew his acquaintance with such a courtly gentleman. So obliging and such felicity that we happened to be here to meet him, do you not agree?" asked Augusta.

Everyone agreed wholeheartedly except for Catherine who had some reservations about how forward her family had been and what expectations may have arisen in the wake of this introduction.

Chapter 10

When the date arrived for Duncan Woulff to visit Rathclare Hall, her mother insisted on joining the party and coaxed Catherine to accompany her but she declined. She was reluctant to bear witness to the fawning attentions she knew would be paid to their visitor and was happy to spend the day in her study. She was especially grateful to have made the choice when a servant appeared carrying a second letter from Colonel Fitzwilliam; at least she was blessed with privacy and no prying eyes when she sat down to read it.

Dear Miss Carteret,

My mission to explore the saga of the pirate queen, Grace O'Malley, has proven to be an exhilarating adventure and one I trust will be of rousing interest to you and animate your imagination of history unfolding beyond the pages of books and written accounts. I believe, Madam, that you will be delighted with the results of my exploration and I carry with me a gift bequeathed to you from an O'Malley descendant. Be not uneasy that said gift creates any obligation on your part for it was given in admiration of your abiding interest in historical events and gratitude for keeping memories alive centred on the achievements of uncommon women of which you are one.

I beg your indulgence that I am not including a full accounting of what I have learned; I am determined that there will be greater felicity if I am present when I relay this remarkable story and can enjoy your response in person. I will, however, share something of my journey.

We left Waterford and made stops at Cork and Bantry Bay before passing the Moher Cliffs which tower over the West Clare coast. Legend has it that a local fisherman was at sea one day and saw a beautiful mermaid sitting on the rocks with whom he struck up a conversation. He distracted her and managed to snatch her magical cloak and returned home to hide it but since the mermaid required the cloak to return to the sea, she was forced to follow him home where he bargained with her to marry him, promising he would some day return the cloak. She agreed but after much searching, her persistence was rewarded; she finally discovered the hidden cloak and escaped back to the sea never to see her husband again.

Regretably, I must report that I have seen neither vampires nor mermaids on my journey and we arrived in Connacht without encountering any pirates, but here I shall leave off this tale until I see you again. We travel overland from Sligo following River Shannon down to Athlone where Grace's son,

Tibbot, was once held prisoner. From there we travel east to Dublin anticipating a journey of approximately two weeks. Be assured I will not delay calling upon you so that I can deliver the memento that once belonged to the Pirate Queen of Connacht.

I remain your humble servant,
Colonel Edward Fitzwilliam

Catherine allowed the letter to fall to her lap and, although vexed at the incomplete chronicle of his journey and the dangled hint of an O'Malley keepsake which she was impatient to see, she had to smile at the contents and the person who wrote it. Colonel Fitzwilliam never failed to amuse and yet still strike an affectionate cord she could not deny in her unguarded moments, for he was always effortlessly diverting.

She hid the correspondence in her room before her mother returned and listened patiently to the effusive approbation of the gathering at Rathclare Hall that included her former tutor, Duncan Woulff, who expressed his sincerest disappointment at her absence, and surely she must regret having missed the convivial conversation that proceeded. A gentleman from the continent who had lived in Rome for so long added such refreshing observations and delightful commentary to any conversation, and he was greatly esteemed for his efforts to teach Mary, who was already showing excellent progress. Augusta was delighted to have him as a regular visitor, as were her many friends who came to call when he was likely to be present, and she had already invited him to attend the ball she was planning when the Bertrams returned, and everyone was eager to hear if there was any news from Colonel Fitzwilliam regarding his arrival back in Dublin. Catherine chose to stay silent on this subject for the time being, wishing to enjoy her privacy a little longer. Later that evening in her room she pulled the letter out again for a fresh reading of its contents.

"A little bird told me you received a letter today," commented Birdie when she entered the room to help Catherine prepare to retire for the night.

"Was it from your colonel, Miss?"

"Pray, do not vex me, Birdie. He is not 'my' colonel but, to answer your question, yes, I did receive a very intriguing letter from him," as she tucked it away in her dressing table.

"Intriguing is it? How very mysterious. Are you eager for his return then?" asked Birdie.

"Only in so far as I wish to hear more about his journey and to receive a token he promised to deliver that once belonged to a pirate queen."

"Oh, Miss, he is bringing you a gift? Your mother will be over the moon."

"I shall have to drag her back to earth then," replied Catherine. "Besides, she and my sister-in-law are currently enjoying the company of Mr. Duncan Woulff, my former tutor, who visits often to give Italian lessons to Miss Mary Jameson and seems to have enthralled every woman with whom he comes into contact."

"Including you, Miss?"

"No! While he has a pleasing address, cuts a handsome figure, and is cultured, intelligent and amiable, I find him rather too self-assured and aware of his appeal, striving to please everyone, especially the ladies, which seems a rather obvious conceit that makes me question his character."

"Oh, then it is Colonel Fitzwilliam you admire and I must say I'm glad to hear it. When me mam heard Mr. Woulff called on you recently, she warned me that he had quite a reputation as a ladies' man."

"Birdie, you misunderstand me entirely. I do admire Colonel Fitzwilliam but I assure you there is no attachment and I prefer that you not speak as if there is. As to Mr. Woulff, hold your tongue with idle gossip from the servants' quarters if you please."

"Yes, Miss. As you wish, Miss."

Chapter 11

The reprieve from multiple social engagements ended with the return of Sir Thomas and Lady Bertram to Rathclare Hall. They came to call at the Park attended by Augusta and Mary Jameson shortly after their arrival back in Dublin. The disdain Catherine felt as she listened to the vain boasting of her cousin, Elizabeth, and observed the prideful preening of her husband, who was obviously besotted with his young wife, required a placid countenance so as not to display her aversion to their prattling.

"Is it not the most elegant lace you have ever seen?" boasted Lady Bertram as she displayed the trim on her neckline that formed a small oval bib with an intricate curving floral motif in the centre that was matched by the decoration on her sleeves. "There is no better place to find such well-designed handwork than from the lacemakers in Belfast. It is made from linen, of course, rather than the less expensive cotton and the needlework is created the way it is done in Venice rather than the crocheted work one often sees here.

"And of all people, who should have noticed and commented upon it? None other than Mr. Duncan Woulff. Such a charming man of fashion with a pleasing address, appealing countenance, and so well informed! When first he glimpsed the trim on my gown he commented on how closely it resembled Venetian lace and he must be allowed to be an excellent judge. Aside from my caro sposo, of course, men commonly take so little notice of these refinements that distinguish one as a person of taste.

"Since Mary began studying Italian with Mr. Woulff, we are all delighted to use those small phrases like 'caro sposo', which of course means 'dear spouse', to add a certain elegance to our conversations. It is ever so continental do you not agree? My sister, Anne, Mrs. Wentworth now, is quite fluent in Italian, but I could never be bothered since Pappa had no interest in visiting that country; he much preferred London society. Had he been interested in travel, I am sure I would have been a great proficient and I do think it is admirable that dear Mary is learning the language before her tour."

Upon hearing this, Catherine could barely maintain her countenance nor could she help but observe that Mr. Woulff had certainly gained a great deal of favour and influence with her cousin and her sister-in-law in the short time they had been acquainted.

Augusta spoke up, "We have decided to turn our party into a masked ball! What a charming element of surprise it will be for our guests and I am sure all our acquaintances will think the scheme ever so elegant. I have taken the liberty of ordering a variety of masks so each guest can make a selection upon arrival and since masks are not a commonly available accessory, I have arranged for them to be sent from London since it would take far too long to secure them from Venice. It will be such a novelty and add an element of mystery during the dancing. Mr. Woulff thinks it is a splendid idea."

While the conversation continued on the topic of planning the grand event, Catherine was able to ask Mary how she was getting on with her tutor and whether he was seeing improvement in her performance.

"Oh, I am making such progress that I wish Mr. Woulff could come every day. He is so kind and supportive that I want nothing more than to please him. He has such fine eyes that sometimes I find them distracting and I lose track of what he is saying, but then I apply myself with even greater diligence to pay attention and gain his approval. Did you find his eyes distracting when he taught you? They are such an unusual colour," she said as she leaned her chin on her hand with a faraway look in her eye.

Catherine had to smile at this reminder of her own youthful feelings about he former tutor and how eager she was to earn his approbation. "I was younger than you at the time and very focused on my studies as I undertook learning more than one language, but Latin was the primary one I studied with him."

"Oh, Latin. It is the foundation of the all the Romance languages such as Italian you know; that is what Mr. Woulff says. How wonderful to study a 'Romance' language do you not think so? Will you wear a mask at the ball? It seems so very romantic does it not? Mr. Woulff will be attending you know; Cousin Augusta invited him and I am so glad that I am out; I do hope he will ask me to be his partner for one of the dances. That would be molto bellissima," Mary sighed.

"Molta bellissima," corrected Catherine and then proceeded to guide a simple conversation in Italian that Mary managed to stumble through while occasionally referencing her dictionary. "You must work on memorising vocabulary, dear, but I will grant that you have made good progress. I am sure your mother will be most impressed when she returns. 'Bravissima'."

Prior to departing, Lady Bertram presented a lovely linen and lace handkerchief to the dowager viscountess whom she knew had such refined taste that the gift would be appreciated for the beauty of the craftsmanship, however, she did not provide one to Catherine as she did not feel her cousin had any interest in such things as fine linens, which was only partially true. In fact, she had influenced her brother to invest in farming flax seed on some of his properties as a means of increasing the wealth of the estate. She was, however, grateful to not be obliged to thank Sir Thomas and his wife for a gift and then be forced to make a fuss over it the way her mother did.

"Arrivederci," sang out the ladies as they left, while Sir Thomas chose a simple 'goodbye' with formal bow.

A little knowledge goes a long to way towards becoming extremely vexing thought Catherine to herself.

* ~ * ~ * ~ *

Catherine spent considerable time examining the ancient scrolls that Mr. Woulff delivered on the day he first visited Rathclare Park, when he became acquainted with Augusta, as well as Mrs. Jameson and Mary, and the decision was made to engage his services as a tutor. Since he frequently visited Rathclare Hall, it came as no surprise when he stopped in one day at Rathclare Park to inquire about her discoveries. She was coming from the greenhouse when he arrived on horseback to greet her and they conversed outside for a time.

"I wanted to check on your progress reviewing the scrolls I delivered and to see if I could be of any assistance," said he. "May I offer to escort you when you're ready to visit Dean Fitzgerald to share you findings? I am eager to hear what you have learned that others might have overlooked."

"I am still very much immersed in the examination of the documents but would be happy to have you accompany me when I have finished which I expect to be very soon. I am afraid social engagements have become more of a distraction lately, much to my regret. I am encourgaged by the progress I see you have made instructing Miss Jameson. She called recently in the company of my cousin, Lady Bertram and her husband, along with my sister-in-law. It seems you have developed quite a loyal following of admiring ladies, all of whom have discovered a newly found interest to learn Italian."

He smiled broadly and answered, "Such charming women; it seems to amuse them to dabble in using a few phrases of the language, but Miss Jameson is very intent upon learning although she is not nearly as adept a student as you were. Then again, few could be, for you have a natural gift that is very unique."

"I try to apply it in useful ways much to the chagrin of my mother," she said with a smile. "She would rather I focused on pursuits more aligned with the expectations of society at large and her expectations in particular, but this comes as no surprise to you; she voiced her displeasure to my father often when I was your student."

"Indeed, I remember it very well, but your father was steadfast in his support of you as was your mother in pressing you to develop social graces that lead to marriage prospects. Perhaps she may finally get her wish, for I understand that you have a new suitor, the son of an earl no less, and your entire family seems greatly enthused about the prospect."

The perturbation Catherine felt at that moment was severe. How dare her family speak so openly and invasively about her personal life to someone so wholly disconnected from her as this former tutor whom she had not seen in years. It was immoderate, intrusive, and unbecoming for a family of rank to spread tales to a visitor from Rome with whom they had all, apparently, become recently enamoured. What could they be thinking and how dare he be so impertinent?

She pursed her lips for a moment and finally replied, "People believe what they wish to believe, all evidence to the contrary."

"Then it is not true?" he asked sounding pleasantly surprised.

She wondered at this slight change in demeanour, as though he was relieved, and an ever so slight shift in his gaze that she could not quite comprehend. It was one of her shortcomings, reading the reactions of others; her introverted nature and social awkwardness made it difficut for her to understand the nuanced responses of people, especially in social settings.

"What is true is that I am not attached nor do I intend to become attached to any prospective suitor; marriage is a condition that I have never sought nor have I any intention to do so in the future."

"Ah," he replied with a warm smile. "Perhaps you have yet to meet the right person then. Surely marriage would provide greater freedoms than you have now and give you the opportunity to experience other places, to pursue your interests, to awaken longings that may have been suppressed."

"I perfectly comprehend what you are suggesting, but there are no circumstances under which I will ever become the possession of another person nor sacrifice my independence and my fortune on the altar of marriage."

Mr. Woulff nodded politely to this response and suggested they go to her study to discuss the ancient scrolls she had been examining before he returned to Trinity. She breathed a sigh of relief when he left. Was it her imagination or had his discourse revealed intentions to court her himself? Was it possible? Had there been a strange shift in the moon or the alignment of the stars and planets, a subtle alteration that was thrusting her into a strange new orbit contemplating life changes she had foresworn all her life? One thing was certain, that if Mr. Woulff had any amorous intentions, they would no longer be directed towards her. She was also perfectly convinced that any interest on his part was most assuredly predicated on the size of her inheritance rather than the attractiveness of her person.

Chapter 12

A note arrived at Rathclare Park the following week announcing the return of Colonel Fitzwilliam and his intention to call that afternoon. To Catherine's great relief, the note had escaped her mother's notice because she was gone already to visit Augusta and discuss plans for the upcoming ball. The date had not yet been determined but would be settled on quickly once her family learned of the colonel's return to Dublin. She found herself quite eager to hear about his exploits and especially to discover what O'Malley treasure he carried with him for her. She had been intrigued ever since receiving his last letter about the token from a descendant of Grace O'Malley, which she miraculously kept hidden from her mother, knowing she would be hounded relentlessly by her entire family to share the contents. They were already overtly preoccupied with speculation about his intentions and the fact that he was carrying a gift for her would only serve to confirm their assumptions. With his arrival, she knew she would be unable to avoid the situation any longer, since they had been awaiting word of his return to set the date of the masked ball.

It was unusual for her to experience a flutter in her stomach when his arrival was announced and he was shown into the drawing room, a sensation she dismissed as over-eagerness to see the promised gift. He entered in high spirits, his complexion tanned by the sea voyage and time spent on the road, a broad smile across his lips when he greeted her. He asked after her mother and being informed that she was gone for the afternoon, his expression became even more animated.

"Pray, give my regards to your mother and express my disappoinment at missing her but, truth be told, I am delighted to find you at home alone. My odyssey may not have taken as long as Homer's tale of the travels and travails of Odysseus, but I think you will find it engrossing enough to be glad to hear of it privately and without interruption. Forgive me if I am being presumptuous."

"No, indeed, I am quite in agreement that the timing is fortuitous. I much prefer to hear your tale in private knowing that it will be repeated again when my family learns of your return for they will insist on hearing all for themselves. As it happens, I have managed to keep private your second letter sent from Connacht, so your arrival will be unexpected and speculation on the gift you carry has been avoided, but their eagerness to learn about your travels is avidly discussed and your return has been highly anticipated."

"By you as well or so I hope, unless your only interest is in the gift I carry?" he replied with a smile.

"Your return is most welcome, gift or none," she replied,

"for I am sure your stories will be most enthralling and I am eager to listen."

"Then I must begin on the day the ship departed Dublin Bay catching the outgoing tide early in the morning on a cloudless day with a light wind out of the west and calm seas at the start. We rounded the tip of the bay at Dalkey heading south and sailed past Bray where we first caught a glimpse of the Wicklow Mountains which I hope to explore some day, for the view from the ship was captivating and I am certain the prospect from the mountains looking down towards Wicklow and the sea must be equally enchanting. We steered our course following the coast and passing by the inlet at Wexford, ran across higher winds and rougher seas before reaching Waterford by evening tide. Ireland has much to offer the traveller seeking the serenity of both pastoral and coastal vistas; one can easily forget the ongoing hostilities that have existed throughout its history long before the English crown claimed this land, and still ongoing to this day; there can be brief respites from all the rebellious clashes and endless bloodshed that have shaped this country, when contemplating one of its sublimely beautiful vistas. That very first day I thought of you in a new light, as the muse to my travels that set me on my journey, the whisperer of questions to ask and knowledge to seek, the silent guide pulling me towards unknown lands and new adventures."

Catherine felt the colour rise in her cheeks at this unexpected tribute and knew not how to respond, until finally she ventured to say, "I had no idea when we met in Bath that my mention of Grace O'Malley would plant a seed that would flourish in such unexpected ways, but I am happy that it inspired your intrepid spirit to undertake such a daunting quest; pray tell me all you learned."

"I travelled with two former compatriots, Billy O'Larkin and Tom Connelly, both of whom I met when I was first stationed in Dublin in 1796 and they were sent to Bantry Bay when notice came the French fleet was sighted and an invasion was thought imminent. Later they helped put down the United Irishmen's Uprising against the Ascendency in 1798 and have served as protection for various government officials over the years; they are able men and familiar with the western terrain, people, and customs. They were more than mildly amused by the reason for my voyage, to explore the history of a pirate queen from two centuries ago, but they are adventurous men and knew how to engage the local residents to scout for trouble and uncover points of interest. It was during a visit to a pub in Waterford that Billy discovered the story of the local vampire, the Dearg Dur, and where to find her burial site. They were quite persuaded after a few pints that they could provoke an encounter with her and were willing to risk their lives by arousing her anger, but she was not induced by their methods to make an appearance despite their best efforts.

"For myself, the Waterford manufacturing site was much more diverting and I greatly enjoyed observing the processes and craftsmanship that create such brilliant and beautiful crystal. The furnaces burn hot and the work is exacting; items are as easily destroyed at any step along the way as delivered complete and breathtakingly beautiful, projecting prisms of colour whenever a light source hits the facets. Luxury items few can afford, produced with a combination of sweat and prowess, but the final products are captivating to behold.

"Please do not be importuned by my decision to bring back a small offering to my muse," he said and pulled from the pocked of his coat a small crystal drop cleverly attached by silver wire to a cone-shaped, silver holder decorated with a delicate filigree design and hanging from a silk cord. "I thought to present it now, so it might gain some favour, before your anticipation of the other gift that I carry from Connacht overshadows it. Be assured that accepting this tribute creates no obligation on your part; you might consider hanging it in the window of your study to refract the light from the sun in that room and remind you of the adventure you inspired. Having never seen your study, I can't know how it is situated but I dare to presume it has windows to the outside world."

Catherine reached out her hand and began to examine the crystal carefully. It was a curious object, beautifully designed, oval in shape, about the size of her thumb, casting prisms of colour when she held it to the light. "You are correct, Colonel, my study does have windows that let it late morning light. Perhaps you would care to see where I spend so much of my time and you can continue the story of your journey from there." She arose and led the way to a nearby room with windows shuttered, which she moved to open and let in the light. There she held up the crystal and saw brightly coloured rainbows refracted throughout the room.

The study was small and cluttered with papers, old books, manuscripts, ancient scrolls, several magnifying glasses, and pens with ink pots. The walls were covered with ancient maps and here and there were fragments of sculptures, obscure rocks, and small statues collecting dust. There were three small storage chests containing multiple drawers with little round knobs and a desk near the window, which was the primary source of natural light, held two glass lanterns to provide additional illumination. The air was thick with the musty scent of dust and old parchment and across from the desk was a chair where she invited him to sit.

"I keep the room closed up much of the time to prevent sunlight from fading the maps but I shall have to reconsider letting in the morning light through the east window if I am to enjoy the gift you have presented to me," said Catherine. "Hitherto, I have never aspired to be a muse to anyone, but one does not choose such a role nor can one argue with the misapprehesion someone else imposes on you, so if it pleases you to place me on such a pedestal, it is your own imaginative doing. Considering the threat of the Dearg Dur that you risked in Waterford, I shall enjoy contemplating that bit of lore and the delightful display of colour your gift adds to my study. Thank you, Colonel." She set the prism aside on her desk and leaned forward expectantly for him to continue his story.

"From Waterford we made a stop at Banfry Bay and engaged the services of a gaelic-speaking, waggish charmer, Paddy Doyle, who regaled us with ribald stories of Irish folklore for the price of a good supply of whiskey and a ride home to Sligo where he promised to provide translation services with the Irish speaking locals. Had you been with us, we would have had no need for the man," said the colonel with a sly smile and a raised eyebrow, "but he was a mightily entertaining addition to our party."

Catherine felt her cheeks colour.

"We rounded the southern most tip of this fair country to encounter the far more rugged Atlantic coast and sailed north to the Burren where we came in view of the magnificent Cliffs of Moher. The insignifance of man compared to these giant sea cliffs and the briny power of ocean waves slamming against them for eons, is humbling and exalting all at once. They run some 14 kilometres along the coast and rise as much as 120 metres at Hag's Head in the south, and reach well over 200 metres further north, where an ancient fort still overlooks the Aran Islands. Such an impressive sight is difficult to adequately describe and I will take no more time except to say that from there we had our first view of our destination, the Province of Connacht. Once the home of two High Kings of Ireland, it is an area so remote that it was a Gaellic stronghold beyond English control until the Tudor conquest in the 1500's. The thought of Grace O'Malley reigning supreme, raiding and plundering passing sea traffic for 30 some years, becomes all the more astounding in view of the ruggedness of this coastline, and the uncommon leadership she must have demonstrated, to earn scores of men as loyal followers, the ire of English magistrates, and most improbably, the respect of the Queen of England."

Catherine could not hold back a look of satisfaction and gratification at this affirmation of history and folklore combined, the consequence of a trifling story shared as a benign remark to a new acquaintance at a social gathering in

Bath many months ago; now unexpectedly resurrected by this unprepossessing gentleman, valiantly pursuing the history of an obscure woman from two centuries earlier, who was the antithesis of the collective expectations of society; a pirate, a warrior, a leader, a woman of consequence in a world that considered women to be of little consequence. There was much to be admired about this adventurous, curious man, an unexpected challenge to her carefully crafted view of men as self-centred and patriarchal.

Unable to contain her curiosity, Catherine asked, "How came you to determine the next steps of your investigation? Had you indentified a local village to make inquiries? Was she a well known figure or long forgotten except by a few kinsmen?"

"As fate would have it, Paddy was a most resourceful companion with a bounty of knowledge about local folklore of his own; a clever imp of a man with an engaging address and a nose for sniffing out information by way of an amiable offer of a pint here and a pint there; an advantageous hire was he, I can assure you. We pulled into Galway Bay and disembarked at the most significant town in the province, where we received our first important intelligence about the existence of Granuaile's Castle on Clare Island in Clew Bay, one of the principal strongholds of the O'Malley clan and the chosen residence of Grace O'Malley.

"We immediately determined to make our way north to County Mayo and find Clare Island which is a mountainous island guarding the entrance to Clew Bay and said to be part of the vast land holdings of the O'Malley family. Many believe

Grace is buried in the Clare Island Abbey, which contains the O'Malley family tomb and has rare medieval roof paintings, as we found out when we visited, but the exact location of her resting place is unknown."

"How came you to discover the family tomb and the roof paintings?" asked Catherine.

"Paddy struck up a conversation with the caretaker in charge of the castle property for many decades, a family role he inherited, who greatly enjoyed the attentions of our party and was more than happy to spin tales to entertain us, although there is no way of ascertaining the veracity of his stories. Clare Island is sparsely populated and the castle is no longer inhabited, but he took great delight in regaling us with the oral history of the area and grew ever more animated as he talked about the pirate queen, for he rarely enjoys such rapt attention from an eager audience. He was quite astounded by our interest, even more so when he learned it was the purpose of our trip. Whether that encouraged embellishments to his account and caused him to spin yarns beyond common knowledge cannot be determined, but never was a man more grateful to perform for such attentive listeners, with Paddy metering out draughts of whiskey to invigorate him. I see your mind at work wondering what great intrigue we uncovered from our host regarding Grace. I shall not importune you for long but must beg your patience to provide some measure of her family's history gathered on the island.

"Her father, Owen O'Malley, came from a long line of ancestors who derived their living from the sea and built fortresses overlooking Clew Bay to exact 'tributes' from ships passing through their territory. The story goes that as a young girl, Grace pleaded with her father to allow her to accompany him on a voyage but he refused, claiming her long hair would get tangled in the lines, after which she cut her hair and dressed like a boy to sneak on board. From then on she was allowed to sail with him and was an experienced seafarer by the age of sixteen when she married her first husband. She was married twice but gossip on the island says between two marriages, she fell in love with a shipwrecked sailor who had washed ashore on the island and, after caring for him, the two became lovers. I will say no more on this topic for now except that the story was corroborated later in the trip."

"Married at sixteen," commented Catherine. "One wonders how she managed to live a life at sea and still raise the son that she had to ransom from Queen Elizabeth."

"Throughout our travels, one of the most frequently repeated stories regarding Grace had to do with her giving birth to that very son on board her ship, and then appearing on the main deck, shouting invectives to rally her troops and turn the tide in a battle with pirates. Quite extraordinary when you think of it," commented Fitzwilliam.

"And you heard this remarkable story repeated by others besides the caretaker on Clare Island? I'm afraid my family's ideas of womanhood will be overthrown completely and their discomposure will be great with these tales of a woman of action demonstrating such vulgar independence, which they will surely find bewildering. Pray tell who else supplied you this intelligence?"

"Ah, that will take us to the source of the gift I carry from the 2nd Marquess of Sligo, an intelligent, energetic, extravagant young man, and a direct descendant of Grace O'Malley, whom we met in Westport."

"A marquess?" gasped Catherine. "A descendant of the pirate queen? I am all astonishment!"

The expression on Colonel Fitzwilliam's face manifested his immense pleasure at the shock and wonder evident on her face. If ever there was a reward for the expedition he had undertaken, it was surely the palpable amazement expressed by his chosen muse, the woman who inspired his mission. His delight was directly proportional to the degree of her surprise.

Chapter 13

"After visiting Clare Island we made our way to Westport where we learned that the Marquess of Sligo resided at Westport House which was built on the foundations of one of the O'Malley fortresses. I sent a note requesting an opportunity to call at the residence and received an immediate invitation to dine the next day with Howe Peter Browne, the 2nd Marquess of Sligo.

"He is a young man in his early twenties, good humoured, energetic, and loquacious; his friendly manners matched his open and welcoming invitation. When he learned of the reason for my expedition to Clew Bay he was excessively delighted; he is well travelled, a lover of history, and took great satisfaction in discussing his family connection to Grace O'Malley.

"You will be interested to know that Grace's son, Tibbot Burke, went on to become the 1st Viscount Mayo, some years after her death. Tibbot married Maeve, the daughter of his jailer, Donal O'Conor, produced eight children, and was knighted Sir Tibbot ne Longe Burke in 1603, the same year that Grace O'Malley and Queen Elizabeth died. Maud, the daughter of Tibbot's son, Miles, and the great-granddaughter of Grace married John Browne III.

"The Browne family arrived in Mayo in the sixteenth century, and their descendants managed to survive the vicissitudes of English rule to expand their estate and transform an old O'Malley fortress into Westport House around 1767. It was designed by the acclaimed architect, William Leeson. The third Earl of Altamont, who became the 1st Marquess of Sligo in 1800, planted trees, created a lake, converted a dusty old village into the prosperous town of Westport and built a thriving linen industry."

"How came the title of Marquess of Sligo rather than Mayo?" asked Catherine.

"Apparently there was already a Marquess of Mayo so Sligo to the north was chosen instead."

Catherine leaned forward expectantly but said nothing more. Surely the marquess was the source of the gift and she trusted Colonel Fitzwilliam would not prolong the story knowing how great was her anticipation.

"I know how eager you are for the unveiling of the gift but bear with me a moment more and I will satisfy your curiosity. My host knew a great deal about Grace O'Malley's family history. When she was married at sixteen to Donal O'Flaherty she was already an experienced seafarer. She bore him three children before he was ambushed and killed by rivals while hunting, who then advanced on his castle believing it to be an easy target with only a woman to defend it. She fought so fiercely and drove them off to protect her brood, that the castle was renamed 'Hen's Castle'. Later she married Richard Burke, a wealthy landowner and chieftain, whose lands allowed her to expand her shipping operations, providing numerous inlets from which she could launch her fleet that included some thirty ships and three galleys; they were used for trade as well as exacting tributes from ships enterig her territory. 'Iron Richard' Burke was the father of Tibbot.

"I asked my host what he knew of the story we heard on Clare Island about Grace having an affair with a shipwrecked sailor. His face lit up with excitement and he excused himself for a few minutes, returning shortly carrying a small wooden box which he claimed once belonged to his ancestor, whom even he referred to as 'the pirate queen'. It contained three tarnished silver buttons and a note that was believed to be in Grace's handwriting saying 'The heart of Philip Grenville'.

"A sailor did wash ashore from a shipwreck on Clare Island; a strong gale had blown his ship off course and it had shattered on the rocks. All died save him and he was brought to Grace more dead than alive, nearly drowned, with severe injuries. It is believed that she nursed him back to health and they began an affair during his recovery. Based on the name on the note, he may have been related to Sir Richard Grenville, a plantation owner in Munster, and also a seafarer and adventurer who sailed to North America as well as fought the Spanish Armada in the Azores. Legend has it that she wished to marry Philip and share her command on the high seas but he rejected the life she offered as unsuitable for his noble English heritage. When he was well enough to travel and bade her farewell, she cut the silver buttons from his leather jerkin that rested above his heart so she would always have his heart with her.

"Sir Howe was so impressed with your knowledge of his ancestor and grateful that you keep her memory alive and shared it with me when first we met, he asked me to carry this gift and present it to you."

With that, Colonel Fitzwilliam reached into his pocket and withdrew a small leather box with a tiny gold hook and eye closure and handed it to Catherine. She reached for it and examined it carefully before sliding the small latch and opening the box to expose the object inside, a small silver button. She was mesmerised holding it up to the light to look at its tarnished silver and scalloped edges. She looked from the button to his eyes, bright with excitement with a broad smile across his face. She returned his smile with her own, something that she rarely did on any occasion; it was heartfelt and warm.

"I am all amazement," she finally said, "that he would part with a family heirloom or even that it survived to this day through so many generations. How was it handed down? Was he not reluctant to give it up?"

"I asked the same question and was told it was greatly esteemed and prized by the female line of the family. It passed through Mile's daughter into the hands of sisters, wives, and daughters. It fell into the keeping of the Browne family with the marriage of John to Maud. It is remarkable that the box and note came intact through all those generations; even more remarkable that the current descendant treasures the history and significance it represents.

"As to why he wished to bestow it on you, he replied that he still had two others remaining and he wanted to pay tribute to you, an independent woman much like his ancestor. He is a high spirited, intellectual gentleman with an open, generous nature; you would find him as interesting as he is charming and you have an open invitation to visit if ever you are in that part of the country. He was quite fascinated by my description of you. When I mentioned your linguistic skills he recalled that Grace was an educated woman who spoke several languages and was fluent in Latin, Spanish, and French; an amazing feat considering her early history at sea. I expect she learned some languages as the result of the need to parley trades and it is said she spoke Latin when she met with Queen Elizabeth to negotiate for her son's release from prison.

"You will appreciate something he told me while we were discussing her second husband, Richard Burke, the father of Tibbot. At the time, ancient Brehan Laws had been in place for centuries in that territory. Those laws viewed women as equal in status to men rather than as property. She made him agree to a one year 'trial' marriage, after which they could decide whether to annul the union. It is said that at the end of the year, she changed the locks on the castle and dismissed him as her husband. However, that may be another questionable part of the legend because they remained together until his death."

"Would that Brehan Laws were still the law of the land affording women more control of their own destinies," replied Catherine. "Certainly Grace O'Malley defined her own destiny when you consider the decades she spent leading men and ruling the seas near her home, and finally settling conflicts between herself and the English magistrates when she successfully negotiated with the Queen of England to release her son. Both women managed to defy the world order dictated by society in their time. Who could imagine he would later became a viscount and a line of descendants would carry the family history forward to this day?

"I can hardly contain my amusement when I think of how aghast my mother will be to hear your story. She was extolling you about the risks of encountering pirates and thieves in pursuit of the legend of a pirate queen, and you return having met her descendant, the Marquess of Sligo, carrying a silver button that once belonged to her English lover. I shall have to strive diligently to maintain my composure when you share this piece of intelligence."

Colonel Fitzwilliam laughed out loud. "Your observations never fail to amuse me. Indeed, your brother was also convinced my journey was folly and would lead to nothing but uncovering a few scruffy papists claiming to be long lost relatives."

"I must give you fair warning that your return will set in place a cascade of events that invite your participation. Since your departure, Sir Thomas and Lady Bertram have arrived for an extended trip to celebrate their wedding and are staying at Rathclare Hall. A masked ball has been planned in their honour as my family is suddenly enamoured with the idea that wearing Italian masks will add to the felicity of the event, and your attendance has been eagerly anticipated. Since you attended Sir Thomas at his wedding, I am sure you will be happy to renew his acquaintance, but, unless you make your escape from Dublin very soon, it will be difficult for you to politely avoid the invitation."

"Make my escape?" said he. "I can think of nothing that would give me more pleasure than to attend, especially if I can claim the first two dances with you, Madam."

"I confess that I rarely dance at such occasions but will make an exception for you. As your muse, how can I refuse, considering the gifts you took the trouble to carry with you? The curiosity about your journey will provide an eager and attentive audience as soon as a dinner can be arranged. They will insist on seeing the silver button, that is unavoidable, but if you don't object, I will keep your second letter private to avoid vexing my mother for withholding it. The prism I shall hang in the window of my study so it is unavoidable that it may be noticed sooner or later, but I do not wish to excite conjecture by my family of a more serious connection by announcing it as a gift to your 'muse'. I do hope you understand."

"I am at your service and will leave all to your discretion. It will remain my private pleasure to have observed the look of surprise on your face today, for I am sure your composure will be fully contained when I tell my story to a larger audience. I understand your apprehension about your family and am all the more grateful to have had a private audience with you this afternoon. It has been a gratifying day, indeed."

Chapter 14

The announcement that Colonel Fitzwilliam had returned to Dublin set about a flurry of activity in anticipation of the masked ball. An invitation to dine at Rathclare Hall was immediately forthcoming and Catherine found herself the centre of unwanted attention when she arrived with Colonel Fitzwilliam and her mother. They were greeted by Augusta and Charles, Mrs. Jameson and her daughter, Mary, as well as Sir Thomas Bertram and his wife.

Sir Thomas was delighted to greet the friend who stood up for him at his wedding to Elizabeth Elliot and boasted rather too loudly that he would be much obliged to return the favour should the need arise. The offer was politely dismissed as unwarranted by the colonel but left Catherine feeling singularly importuned by the impertinence of the remark and the knowing glances that passed around the room. At last the topic changed to Colonel Fitzwilliam's trip to Waterford and his quest to learn more about the pirate queen, Grace

O'Malley. Everyone knew that a gift to Catherine was involved but she had refused to provide any information from their meeting in her study, much to her mother's consternation, insisting that the family must wait until they were gathered together and all would be revealed directly from the source.

Colonel Fitzwilliam began by describing the voyage to Waterford and his visit to the crystal factory which drew an elated response from the viscount and his wife who talked about the delightful punch bowl they had acquired and how wonderfully useful it would be at the upcoming masked ball. Mary was much more interested in the story of the Dearg Dur that he had written about in his letter, asking for more details, wondering what the burial site was like, and whether his companions had truly guarded his room that night. A distracted Lady Bertram examined the lace on her cuffs but her husband gave his avid attention to the story; as a man who had sailed as far as Antiqua, he enjoyed tales of adventure. Charles expressed his approval of the colonel's choice of companions as he still was convinced that there was danger in the wilds of western Ireland for a man of consequence, who would require protection, and smugly held the opinion that chasing the legend of a pirate queen was a fool's errand.

The party's attentiveness was secured by the time the visit to Clare Island was revealed. It was clear that the O'Malley family had wielded power over a large area of Connacht, both by land and sea. They were traders deriving their living mainly by the sea and exacting tributes from passing ships in their territorial waters; they were not outlaw pirates pillaging wherever they could although they were known to do some raiding in Spain.

The story of Grace cutting her hair and sneaking on board for her first voyage with her father shocked the ladies and Mary commented that she would be too frightened to do such a thing and was far too attached to her lovely, long hair that often attracted compliments, to consider cutting it off.

The description of Granuaile's Castle on Clare Island and the O'Malley family tomb with rare medieval roof paintings garnered up a new level of respect for the historical significance of a family dynasty that would erect such a remarkable memorial. When the discussion turned to the story by the old caretaker about a shipwrecked sailor who was taken as a lover by Grace, the ladies all gasped with shock and disbelief, certain the tale was meant to provoke, especially in light of the drink provided to encourage expansive storytelling by the caretaker. Surely it was meant to add a scandalous enhancement to her legend.

"Perhaps Mary should be excused from the room," said the dowager viscountess. "She need not be exposed to stories of seduction at her young age. I hope there will be no more mention of such immoral behaviour in your account, Colonel."

"I'm afraid I cannot make such a promise," he replied, "for I have yet to tell you all that I learned from his descendant on this matter."

"Oh, please," begged Mary, "don't dismiss me. I'm sixteen and quite old enough to hear of such matters; Grace O'Malley was married at my age and fought pirates after giving birth on board her ship, and we've already learned about a bloodthirsty vampire in Waterford; this can hardly be worse." Her mother, Mrs. Jameson, nodded in agreement and the young lady was allowed to stay.

Colonel Fitzwilliam continued his narrative, saying they learned of a descendant of Grace O'Malley who lived in Westport from the old caretaker on Clare Island so that became their next destination. The shock and surprise expressed on every face in the room when they learned that Howe Peter Browne, 2nd Marquess of Sligo, was a direct descendant of Grace O'Malley, was anticipated by Catherine; she'd experienced it herself. They were enthralled with the description of Westport House built on the remains of an O'Malley fortress, with its lake and woods and bustling village thriving with the linen industry. All thoughts of a coarse pirate queen were quickly displaced by the ascent of the family, the scale of the estate, and the description of the charming 2nd Marquess of Sligo; a direct line descendant of Grace O'Malley's son, Tibbot, who emerged from prison on the orders of Queen Elizabeth after his mother negotiated his release. That he went on to become a viscount was a tribute to the status and influence the O'Malley clan had achieved in the western province of Connacht; that his family now claimed the rank of marquess and eclipsed the Dalrymple's rank of viscount did not go unnoticed.

"Clearly I misapprehended the legacy of her legend," admitted Charles with a note of surprise. "What a splendid outcome of your journey to discover a man of rank and property with whom you could affirm the verity of the folklore based on real historical evidence. Pray, tell us of the gift the marquess sent for Catherine? She has been reticent to share any intelligence about it although that is in keeping with her character. We are all eager to find out what you carried back from your journey. Does it have any historical signifance?"

"I shall not venture to speak to the historical significance," replied the colonel. "Its value is in the eye of the beholder, is it not?" as his gaze came to rest on Catherine along with that of everyone in the room. "Madam, would you care to reveal the gift?"

Catherine had been both dreading this moment and yet revelling in it, knowing the tremor of shock that would follow. It would excite much prognostication about her relationship with the colonel, but that was unavoidable, and it would be dismissed by her as an insignificant token from a man she had never met, delivered by a man whose visit to Ireland would soon be ending. She pulled out her indispensible, opened the drawstrings, and removed the small leather box. There was a gasp in the room for it surely looked designed to hold a ring. She carefully opened the clasp, removed the silver button, and held it up to view.

"Whatever is that?" demanded her mother. "What is it you hold in your hand? Is it a button?"

"You are correct," answered Colonel Fitzwilliam. "Sir Howe validated the story of the shipwrecked sailor and this silver button came from his leather jerkin, cut off by Grace herself. There were three altogether and a note believed to be in Grace's handwriting that said 'the heart of Philip Grenville'; the marquess chose to part with one of them as a tribute to your daughter for keeping his ancestor's memory alive."

"Whatever does it mean?" demanded the dowager viscountess. "The heart of Philip Grenville? What does it mean?"

The colonel proceeded to tell the story of Philip Grenville including the love affair and his decision to return to his family rather than staying with Grace despite her pleas. The day he left her, she took her dagger and cut the three buttons directly over her lover's heart to keep for herself. Her female descendants honoured the memory of her doomed affair by handing the heirlooms down until they came into the care of Sir Howe.

"Oh, how terribly romantic," swooned Mary. "Swept away by love after the sea swept him ashore and into her arms. Truly an affair of the heart held dear by the buttons over his heart."

"My dear child, please contain your effusive extolling of inappropriate liaisons," responded the dowager. "My opinion has been confirmed that you are far too young to hear such stories for they go to your head. Marriage is the only avenue for expressions of love."

"May I please see the button?" asked Mary, ignoring the scolding from her aunt. With that, Catherine handed over the box and it was passed around for all to view.

Lady Bertram suggested that it would be a lovely thing to visit Westport and examine the quality of the linen being produced there and that she would be very well disposed to meet the marquess and his wife by way of introduction from Colonel Fitzwilliam. "One does not want to overlook an opportunity to meet others of rank with whom one might have much in common such as elevated taste and an appreciation of art, and history, of course."

Catherine recoiled at the hubris of the remark but managed to maintain her countenance.

Sir Thomas replied that he could not extend their trip for such a venture as he had business matters awaiting his attention at Mansfield Park to which he must attend, adding, "Perhaps during another visit, dearest." Augusta had a wistful look on her face as did Margaret Jameson.

"What will you do with this precious token?" asked Mary.

"I shall keep it in my study with my other prized antiquities," replied Catherine.

"Oh, I think I should put it on a ribbon and wear it around my neck," sighed Mary.

* ~ * ~ * ~ *

Augusta announced that it was time to adjourn to the dining room where they could continue the discussion and everyone could satisfy their curiosity. There were many questions and much detail shared before the topic was finally retired. After dinner Augusta introduced a new subject about a rumour she heard from a friend that a refined lady with genteel manners was seen in a local Dublin pub accompanied by a courtly gentleman, and that the woman, joining in the revelry exhibited by other patrons, stood up and made a speech in the Irish language which, of course, everyone knows is unlawful to be spoken in public places.

"It is curious that the event occurred just after we met Colonel Fitzwilliam and you arranged to give him a tour of Trinity to see the *Book of Kells*. Such a coincidence is it not?

A lady of rank is rarely seen going into a pub and rubbing elbows with the lower classes let alone making a speech in a forbidden language. Apparently the pub is very near where you are staying in Dublin, Colonel Fitzwilliam. Curious indeed," said Augusta.

Catherine maintained her composure and carefully avoided her mother's glaring eyes and said nothing, grateful that no colour rose in her cheeks to betray her and that her countenance remained unperturbed. Colonel Fitzwilliam conjectured that perhaps a lady of consequence from County Mayo had been visiting in Dublin. "We hired a man from Sligo to accompany us as a translator because the Irish language is spoken so frenquently there. I rather expect that the Marchioness of Sligo is conversant in it although I never thought to ask her. It is very commonly used in that area," he added. "Personally I have heard nothing of the rumour at my accomodations but then I have been travelling." He stole a glance at Catherine but she avoided his eyes as well.

"One would hope that the lady was from another part of the country," remarked Charles. "Making a spectacle of oneself in a pub would break all bounds of propriety by any local lady from our social circle."

The conversation then turned to the upcoming masked ball, introducing a much more lively discussion. The colonel asked how they came upon the unique idea and Augusta responded, "Catherine's former tutor, Mr. Duncan Woulff arrived for a visit from Rome and Mrs. Jameson hired him to teach Mary the Italian language in advance of their grand tour that will take them to Italy next spring. It inspired the idea of having a ball in the Venetian style to add a unique ambiance to the event."

"He is a wonderful tutor and taught me so much more than just the language; about the culture and customs of Italy as well," enthused Mary. "Everyone has been captivated by him and all the ladies who visit began using Italian words and phrases and then my aunt had the extraordinary idea to acquire Venetian-style masks for the ball. It will be so exotic to wear them and dance, without knowing whom your partner is."

"To be sure it is but a lark, a bit of fun to add an element of mystery and surprise," said Augusta. "The masks have just arrived and are divine; it will be such a delight to see our guests make their selections and model their choices. I do hope you will partake in the sport, Colonel."

At home that evening, Catherine found her mother to be most seriously importuned. "Do not play the innocent with me," demanded her mother. "Your prideful independence has gone too far. I have no doubt that the scheme was all your doing; Colonel Fitzwilliam would never transgress social mores by inviting you to a pub for you to make an indecent display of yourself. Do not deny it! Were it any other man I would terminate the relationship for such a betrayal of my trust, but perhaps that was also part of your plan, to have me dismiss a potential suitor. You are an obstinate, headstrong woman, Catherine, and it will not serve you well to jeopardise an opportunity for an alliance with a gentleman of rank who obviously holds you in high regard despite your indifference. You would be a fool to throw away potential happiness in favour of a lonely existence with your precious dead languages and dusty scrolls."

Catherine made no defence, excused herself, and retired to her room.

Chapter 15

"You look quite fetching tonight, Miss. I like the dress your mother had made for you. It is a lovely, creamy silk, and the beige embroidery is elegant. It suits you very well," said Birdie.

"Thank you, Birdie. I suppose I must be grateful to my mother since I gave the ball and my attire no thought at all."

"She asked me to pay special attention to dressing your hair as well," said Birdie. "I have this lovely ribbon to plait in it if you have no objection?"

"Do whatever is necessary to get me through a tedious night," replied Catherine.

"A tedious night? How can you say such a thing? After all, you will have the attentions of two eligible men seeking your favour. How will you choose? Colonel Fitzwilliam is an avid suitor and I understand Mr. Woulff will also be in attendance and will surely seek you out."

"Please, Birdie. Do not refer to either man as a suitor, I beg you. I will do my best to avoid all suitors with the exception of having agreed to dance the first two dances with the colonel, but he is well aware that I have no interest in suitors."

"Yes, Miss. Is he the one who gave you the lovely prism hanging in the window of your study? Did he bring it back from his journey, perhaps from Waterford? It's quite lovely and it's nice that you open the windows to your study more often now. Little rainbows reflect all over the walls when the sun is shining through. Has your mother noticed it?"

"You know she rarely enters my study but I suppose she will notice inevitably. Hopefully after he has returned to England."

"And Mr. Woulff? Does he return to Italy soon?"

"Mr. Woulff's plans are none of my concern. He will be attending the ball tonight so perhaps I will learn more then."

"Just as well he's going, Miss. From what I hear, his charms have captivated many of the ladies who cross his path, young and old. The days he tutors Miss Mary at the big house attract all sorts of visitors, I am told."

"What have you heard, Birdie? Is there anything of concern that I should know? You are right that he is admired by many but I certainly hope that no young ladies have been importuned."

"Young or no, he enjoys the admiration from what I hear, and he knows the effect he has."

"Then I hope he will be on his way back to Rome soon. There is no need for heartbreak that may follow in his wake."

* ~ * ~ * ~ *

Upon entering the ballroom of Rathclare Hall, Catherine and her mother moved through the reception line which included Sir Thomas and Lady Bertram, and were then asked to choose between a selection of Italian masks in varying designs of black or white. She reluctantly chose white and tied the ribbon behind her hair hoping earnestly that she would not be required to wear it for long. After the reception line dispersed, Augusta flitted around the room greeting friends and coaxing reticent guests to don a mask, announcing to all that the first two dances required masks after which they could be removed unless they were adding to the personal felicity of the merrymakers.

She made her way to the outskirts of the gathering in hopes of avoiding the usual insipid small talk concerning the size of the room, the elegance of the dresses, the liveliness of the music, and other banalities. A tall, elegantly dressed man wearing a black mask approached saying "Buonasera, Signora," while making a slight bow.

"Ah, Mr. Woulff, I believe you are the cause of this rather extravagant addition of masks to the affair; your influence has expanded beyond tutoring Italian and swept up our hostess with grand ideas for entertaining with a continental flare."

"I cannot deny it," he replied. "It seems the viscountess embraces all things Italian with enthusiasm which has also captivated the interest of many of her very charming friends. I must ask your forebearance; if this was my influence, it was entirely unintentional and I hope that your good opinion of me has not been overthrown. May I say you are looking particularly well tonight in a very becoming dress, and may I be so bold as to claim your hand for the first dance this evening? It would be an honour to escort my former pupil."

"I assure you my good opinion is not so easily overthrown but I have already been claimed for the first two dances," replied Catherine.

"Ah, I see my application comes too late; I am given to understand that your friend has recently returned and can only presume it is he who shall enjoy the privilege?"

"You are correct, sir, the privilege is mine," stated Colonel Fitzwilliam coming up from behind Mr. Woulff.

With that, introductions were made by Catherine with a few polite exchanges between the men, after which Mr. Woulff excused himself and left them to join the rest of the party, where he was greeted effusively by many of the women who had come to know him from frequent visits to Augusta on the days he came to tutor.

As they stood together observing the man whose charm of person and address had captivated the attentions of the viscountess and her friends, Fitzwilliam ventured that the idea of having a masked ball was inspired by his presence.

"I say, there appears to be a great deal of enthusiasm for the wearing of masks this evening. Do you suppose it allows for a new form of flirtation that conceals extravagant admiration behind a disguise?" commented the colonel.

"It is all facade displayed at these events, only in this case, there are masks on top of the usual masks people wear at social functions to disguise their thoughts. It is all pretense," replied Catherine.

"I perfectly comprehend why these functions do not suit

you; you would rather be tucked away in your study or the library down the hall than socialise, and for that I cannot blame you. For myself, I am inclined to be more obliging and hope the engagement will produce some felicity of contact or conversation to make attending an event worthwhile. In this particular case, the opportunity to dance with you again is a very worthy inducement so long as you promise not to turn the wrong direction or step on my feet," he said with a smile. "Shall we? I believe the musicians are about to begin."

As they joined the other dancers, Catherine recognised Mary by the beaming smile on her face as she waited beside her tall, handsome, and elegantly dressed partner, Mr. Woulff, for their turn to promenade down the line.

Catherine managed to avoid invitations other than complying with an offer from Sir Thomas which she felt obliged to honour and finally dancing with Mr. Woulff who entreated her a second time. Colonel Fitzwilliam happily joined the milieu and partnered with his host, Augusta, Lady Bertram, and Mrs. Jameson as did Duncan Woulff who included a second dance with Mary and danced with several of the ladies with whom he was newly acquainted. Meanwhile, the colonel engaged in conversations with many of the gentlemen including the host, Charles. He was as charmingly at ease as Catherine was ill at ease, especially after overhearing conversations about what an eligible suitor the colonel was and what a fine conquest she had made.

Chapter 16

Not long after the masked ball, Colonel Fitzwilliam called one afternoon and invited her to walk in the garden. He was the first to bring up the subject of the party and guests saying, "What an amusing event your brother and his wife planned. I am sure it is the talk of Dublin society; many of the guests continued to wear their masks throughout the evening which must have pleased the viscountess. Your former tutor, Mr. Woulff, was much in demand by the ladies; it would seem his presence cast a rather conspicuous cultural influence on the event. Never have I heard so many Irish-born ladies using Italian phrases to greet friends or express their amusement."

"I can neither argue nor explain; all evidence clearly points to his influence in local society. Since his return from Rome he seems to have a unique ability to charm those who would be charmed by his courtly manners, pleasing countenance, and fashionable attire."

"Are you among those who admires these attributes then?" he asked.

"When I was a girl of twelve or thirteen I admired him greatly but that was because he encouraged my learning, praised my efforts, and I believed he esteemed me; I was grateful for his approbation and appreciated that he expanded the quality of my thinking and world view. He treated me kindly and nurtured my development which provided relief from the unremitting disapproval of my mother. However, I am no longer a precocious ingenue and find myself mildly amused by the conceit of his courtly manners and self-awareness of his effect on ladies of all ages. The first time he visited Rathclare Park, the ladies present almost swooned when he entered the room and the style of his response encouraged it. For myself, I despise arts willfully employed to captivate women who are already susceptible to flattery."

"Save you?"

"I hope that flattery will never be an impulse to which I am susceptible."

"Let us hope many of the ladies are wise enough to recognise that a philanderer in their midst is capable of creating havoc when so much admiration is directed his way by so many."

"Do I detect a note of jealousy? You have also enjoyed the admiration of many in our circle," she laughed.

"My observations are born of mistrust for his character and integrity rather than jealousy, and there is only one person whose approbation I desire."

Catherine could not meet his gaze for a moment and waited until he began the conversation anew.

"Sir Thomas sent a note that they are soon to depart for his estate, Mansfield Park; it seems business requires his attention at home although I believe supporting his lady's expensive tastes and enthusiasm for acquisitions may put a strain on his purse. He takes great satisfaction in exhibiting his beautiful young wife, but her appetite for finery may be insatiable from what I have observed."

"She is vanity personified, as was her father," replied Catherine, "but they seem very well suited to one another; each has a partiality the other fulfills, her beauty and his vigour, yet I hesitate to imagine the impact their combined vanities have on his family and the possibility that they invariably create clashes. Pray I never bear witness to the discord a beautiful, young, vain, second wife brings to an established family. And what of you, Colonel? Has your next adventure taken shape?"

"Madam, may we finally dispense with the formalities by which we address each other? I would welcome being addressed by my given name, Edward, and be priviledged to address you as Catherine. It seems to me that we are friends enough to take that step; after all, I did escort you to a Dublin pub and risk your mother's wrath, not to mention that of your brother. You have been redeemed for the temerity of sharing the legend of Grace O'Malley and inspiring my voyage to Connacht by the gift from her descendant, and I would consider it an honour to be friends with whom we use our given names."

"I agree, Edward. We are friends, let there be no doubt, and privately at least, I welcome you to call me Catherine."

"Regarding my plans," he responded, "I am to embark on my annual visit to Rosings Park, the estate of my aunt, Lady Catherine de Bourgh. I rather dread it this year because my cousin, Darcy, and I usually undertake the trip together but that will not be possible as there has been a rift between them."

"A rift? I hope I am not being impertinent to ask the cause?"

"Our aunt was exceedingly displeased when Darcy married Elizabeth as she considered him unofficially betrothed to her own daughter, Anne. She claims it was both her wish and that of her sister, Darcy's mother, who is now deceased; that they had planned for it at birth that their two children would marry. He took a wife of his own choosing and a remarkably astute choice it was. You have met her, of course. Elizabeth Darcy is an intelligent, witty, and loving companion well suited to him, but Lady Catherine has not forgiven him as yet."

"Mrs. Darcy is a delightful acquaintance; I greatly enjoyed meeting her in Bath; a sensible woman with whom one can carry on a proper conversation. What has become of Anne if I may ask? Has she found another suitor?"

"Indeed, you are looking at him. My father and Lady Catherine have turned their attentions to me now that Darcy is married, and the pressure on both sides is relentless. Hence my reluctance to visit Rosings Park this year without my usual companion as a buffer and facing coercion on two fronts from my family. Had I any attraction to the lady it might be tolerable but she is of a weak constitution, with little information, no interests, and reticent to voice opinions of any kind because her mother is only interested in her own opinions of which she has many. Lady Catherine is a force of nature which leaves little room for her daughter to blossom or grow, even if she were so inclined, and I have seen little evidence of that.

"My father shares the wishes of Lady Catherine that an alignment between the families will advance the wealth of both estates which is his only concern for his second son; affection is not a consideration. He is from a tradition that views marriage as a commercial transaction between families and, once married, a man can do as he pleases and seek affection wherever he wishes so long as he does his duty and sires an heir. The pressure will be great this year for me to take a wife."

"Family pressures regarding marriage can be relentless as I well know. I am fortunate that my situation in life allows me choices that most women do not have. Will you be required to stay long?"

"I usually stay a fortnight which is about as long as I can bear the endless pontification of Lady Catherine, who has an opinion on every subject, expects agreement with every utterance, and demands her share of every conversation. To be sure it will test my patience and fortitude; I shall be grateful to look back on the adventure I've experienced here in Ireland as I have none other to anticipate when I leave."

"I understand that Sir Thomas and his lady depart Rathclare Hall on Saturday next and will stop here to bid us farewell," said Catherine. "My brother and his wife will join them as well as Mrs. Jameson and Mary. Perhaps you would care to call and see them off; I know they would all welcome the opportunity to see you."

"Despite our observations about Sir Thomas and his wife, I have enjoyed his company and would be happy for an opportunity to say goodbye. I shall see you on Saturday."

Chapter 17

Colonel Fitzwilliam arrived at Rathclare Park on the day of Sir Thomas and Lady Bertram's planned departure and was waiting with the dowager viscountess and her daughter in the drawing room when they heard the sound of carriages arriving.

Augusta entered first with her husband, Charles, and Mrs. Margaret Jameson, followed by Sir Thomas and Lady Bertram.

"Where is Mary?" inquired her mother. "I expected her to be here by now; they had a full two hour head start. Mr. Woulff came to bid us farewell at Rathclare Hall before he departs for Rome and Mary asked if she could ride with him here, since he intended to call on you before heading back to Trinity College. I wonder what could be keeping them?"

"We have seen nothing of them this afternoon; only Colonel Fitzwilliam has crossed our threshold today," replied Catherine. "Was there another stop planned before arriving here? I should be glad to see Mr. Woulff as I have some papers he could carry with him to Dean Fitzgerald."

"No other stops were mentioned," replied Margaret, "but I am sure they will be here soon."

Small talk began but in short order the room grew quiet as everyone became aware of the look of distress on Margaret's face who was tapping her fingers nervously on the arm of her chair repeating, "What could be keeping them?" Attempts at casual conversation faded as tension began to build until finally, with creeping suspicion, Catherine excused herself and went to find Birdie.

"Birdie, tell me what you know of the gossip among the servants about Duncan Woulff. I am becoming increasingly uneasy about his relationship with my sixteen-year-old cousin who has yet to arrive here and is in his company. Whatever you have heard, please tell me."

"I am sorry Miss, I know nothing of present times but I heard talk that Mr. Woulff had a dalliance with one of the servant girls while he was your tutor. The girl was young, an upstairs maid at the big house, and was sent away to one of the laundries to work and deliver her baby; it's what becomes of young, unmarried girls who get in trouble. That's all I know."

"Who was the source of this story, Birdie?"

"Me mam, Miss. When she learned of his first visit here, she made the comment to hide away the young girls lest he take a shine to them. I know nothing more, I swear."

Catherine, flushed with anxiety, said, "Then let us go to the kitchen to seek your mother."

Shortly thereafter, she returned to the drawing room, pale

with concern, and sat down beside her mother. "Mamma, tell me what you remember of the dismissal of Mr. Woulff from Father's service as our tutor. Why was he dismissed? I must know all."

"It was so long ago," replied her mother. "I can hardly recall."

"You must, Mamma. Please try."

"There was a young servant, an upstairs maid, who was sent away from our service because she was in the family way. She was Catholic, of course, and flirtatious girls like that that can often give way to their passions; who knows who her partners were? She was sent away to one of the Magdalene laundries to have her illegitimate baby and pay for her sinful ways. There was rumour that Mr. Woulff may have been one of her dalliances but there was no proof; your father decided it was better to terminate his employment than risk a scandal, so he was dismissed. And might I remind you, Catherine, you were devastated by his departure. He was your favourite tutor."

Looks of alarm crossed the faces of all present.

"He had every charm of person and address a man could have and we were so easily captivated by him, Mary most of all; the girl was out of her senses for him. Is it possible Mr. Woulff's scheme has always been to seduce my daughter? It cannot be. He would not dare!" wailed Mrs. Jameson.

Colonel Fitzwilliam spoke up. "Tell us exactly what you remember the last time you saw her. Time is of the essence."

"Mr. Woulff arrived at Rathclare Hall to bid us all goodbye and gather his things. Mary rushed in and begged me to allow her to travel with him in his gig because we were all bound here to see you. I saw no harm in it since they spent a good deal of time together for her lessons, he was leaving to go back to Rome, and she might not see him again until we visit during our tour. She was so devoted to learning the language, you know, and it might be her last chance to practice with him for some time. However, our departure was delayed so they were ahead of us by perhaps two hours. What can he mean by absconding with my daughter? What is his design? Why would he do such a thing?"

"Is there any other detail you can remember?" asked the colonel.

"Only that I noticed a small valise being placed into the gig next to another one, but I presumed it held papers and books from the tutoring sessions."

By this time, the gentlemen were on full alert and the ladies in a state of shock and dismay, all save Catherine who was already formulating a plan. "If his scheme is to elope with Mary, then time is of the essence if they are to be intercepted."

Colonel Fitzwilliam spoke up: "He has few choices: either to hide her away in Dublin and catch the first ship to Bristol to travel overland through England to France; or sail directly to the continent, Spain or Portugal perhaps, and travel by sea through the Gibralter Strait to Italy. The other alternative is to make his way north to Belfast and flee to Scotland where they can marry immediately. The other routes pose a greater challenge and expense if his wish is to claim her through marriage as soon as possible."

"Marry?" exclaimed Margaret. "How is that even

conceivable? He has been directing his attentions to me; I could have married for a second time had I been willing to risk my fortune on a man who would take possession of it the moment the ceremony was complete. And all this time he was toying with my daughter as well? What does he gain from that?"

Catherine replied, "He gains her dowry and any inheritance once the marriage takes place."

"Oh, my dearest, my innocent darling Mary; how can this have come to pass? What can be done to recover her from this scoundrel?"

Colonel Fitzwilliam answered: "Dublin and the shipyard must be scoured to discover them if that was his plan. Viscount Dalrymple, may I suggest you head immediately to Dublin with a note I shall provide that must be handed to the compatriots with whom I travelled to Connacht; they're good men and discreet. They can check passenger manifests and inns where the couple might stay. They probably will not have crossed the channel today or boarded a ship for the continent based on their late start."

"Meanwhile, I shall ride north immediately," said the colonel. "His gig is pulled by a single horse with two passengers so I can make up some of the time by riding hard in pursuit. It is likely they will head for a coaching route to Belfast and abandon the gig at an inn where horses are swapped for fresh ones. If I can intercept them along the way, I will bring her back."

"I insist on joining you, Charles," said Sir Thomas. "There is nothing I abhor more than untrustworthy men seducing young women of rank for their own enrichment. We shall engage your colleagues to help us uncover them if they are there, Colonel."

"Unscrupulous men willing to use their position of influence and trust to seduce young ladies and claim their fortunes is an abomination that I have borne witness to as well," responded Colonel Fitzwilliam. "He must be stopped at all costs."

Catherine interjected, "I will make my way separately to Trinity and find Dean Fitzgerald to uncover what he knows of Mr. Woulff's immediate plans. If anyone has an idea of where Mr. Woulff would head and where he might hide out in Rome, it will be Dean Fitzgerald. I will return here as soon as I learn anything."

"My poor girl; what is to become of her? Foolish child, and more the fool am I for imagining a rogue like Duncan Woulff was interested in me, rather than my fortune or my guileless daughter," moaned Margaret.

"Do not blame yourself, Margaret; she was easier prey than you. Be glad you were wise enough to recognise a fortune hunter and protect yourself from his advances," responded Catherine.

"I should have seen it, right under my nose! She was besotted with him, out of her senses, wild with admiration. I thought it only the infatuation of a school girl but now, look where it has led. He is twice her age! How could I have been so blind?"

Lady Bertram spoke up to say, "Sir Thomas is an excellent judge of character and he often commented that for all his charm, there was something off about Mr. Woulff. I will admit I was delighted by his courtly manners when first I met him, but I came to believe there was an artfullness to his address meant to intentionally captivate women."

"We were, all of us, taken in and my good opinion is completely overthrown," declared Augusta. "His address and manners, the style of his dress, his amiable responses, all were captivating, but I never quite trusted him and only allowed his frequent visits to benefit Mary, and support her interest in learning Italian. Now I must suffer the anquish of self-reproach for introducing the scoundrel into our midst and try to comfort poor Margaret, who left Mary in our charge. I entreat you, do not blame yourself for not recognising his treachery; be thankful you had the wisdom to deny him access to your fortune. If only we can recover dear Mary, all will be righted."

"I said from the outset that the man was not to be trusted," stated the dowager viscountess, "but was overruled as I always am."

Wishing to hear no more, Catherine put on her Spencer and grabbed her bonnet, sent for the carriage, and prepared to depart immediately for Trinity College. Colonel Fitzwilliam had called for his horse and was ready to ride out as well.

"God's speed, Edward."

"Do not lose hope, Catherine. If they have gone north, I will find them and return the young lady to her family. With luck, I shall reach them before he can take further advantage of her if they make an overnight stop on their way to Belfast. I shall return as quickly as I am able."

Chapter 18

When Catherine arrived at Trinity, she raced to Dean Fitzgerald's office, rushing past the secretary in the outer room, and bursting through the door to his chambers.

"Catherine, my dear, what a surprise. I was not expecting you today. Why do you look so flushed? Has something happened? Please do sit down and tell me what brings you here in such a state."

"Forgive me if I importune you, Dean Fitzgerald. I do not wish to alarm you but urgent matters bring me here and I must inquire what you know about Duncan Woulff's whereabouts or immediate plans? There are unfortunate circumstances that he may be party to which require immediate resolution and I must beg your discretion for the information I am about to reveal.

"We have just discovered that Miss Mary Jameson, daughter of my cousin, and lately staying at Rathclare Hall while her mother was away, has disappeared, and we have reason to believe she is accompanied by her tutor, Mr. Woulff, who was hired to help advance her Italian language skills, but may have had more sinister motives in cultivating a relationship with her. She is only sixteen years of age and has gone missing this afternoon; he was to drive her in his gig to Rathclare Park and they failed to arrive. We have just learned that he may have been involved in a past incident where he took advantage of a young girl and now she may be at risk of a deeper involvment in a scheme for him to profit at her expense."

"Oh, my dear, unsettling news, indeed! I wish I could say something to allay your fears, but I myself, have just received disconcerting news about Duncan. It seems he may have been involved in a spurious business activity involving selling forgeries of ancient coins and works of art that have made their way into the hands of wealthy patrons. We have been able to ascertain that recent acquisitions made by him for the college are genuine, but transactions occurring in and around Rome are suspect, and inquiries have been made as to his whereabouts. His arrival here was unexpected but we considered it to be fortuitous because of the treasures he brought with him to add to our collection. Now I am alarmed that he may be attempting to mitigate his transgressions and resulting debts by making an unprincipled connection with a member of your illustrious family. My connection with your dear, departed father, a most honourable man, causes me great apprehension that our institution may be the source of a potential scandal."

"What do you remember of the circumstances under which he was removed as a tutor to Charles and me? I remember distinctly that it was an abrupt departure; that he was released from our service and sent to Rome. Do you know the cause for the dismissal?"

"Your father only indicated that his presence had disrupted the equanimity of the household staff which was hardly surprising; even as a young man he attracted the admiration of the ladies. Nothing specific was said about him and, as it happened, we found placement for him in the acquistions' department of a sister institution and sent him to Rome. There was nothing untoward about the change in his situation and we have worked in a spirit of collaboration ever since. I am dismayed to hear he has taken advantage of a member of Viscount Dalrymple's family. Please convey these sentiments to your brother, who has been such a generous supporter of our department since your father's death. We had no way of knowing he might be an untrustworthy scoundrel or would never have admitted him into our midst. It is very troubling indeed. What has been done to discover them?"

"My brother is searching for them in Dublin to see if they attempt to travel by sea; Colonel Fitzwilliam has ridden out towards Belfast lest they are headed north to reach Scotland."

"Ah. Colonel Fitzwilliam, a good man, one you can count on in a crisis I venture; a man worthy of your attention, unlike Woulff, who might have seen you as a likely target for his deceitful ways, especially if he was in need of money for debts or wrongdoing. I am glad you have a level head and are not easily taken in by such a Lothario as Duncan Woulff. Your colonel is a man of good character and integrity, a much better choice."

With a sigh of exasperation she endeavoured to refocus the discussion. "What do you know of his plans to return to Rome? Would he likely travel by sea or cross country? Did he have other stops planned? Other colleagues to meet during his travels? When was he expected back in Rome? Please, Dean Fitzgerald, tell me all you know that might help us to discover his whereabouts."

"Yes, yes, very well. Let us check to see what my secretary might know; they had a friendly relationship and perhaps he can help. I do believe Duncan came thither by sea."

Chapter 19

When Catherine next saw Edward, Mary Jameson was safely ensconced at Rathclare Hall, having been recovered on the road at an coaching inn, waiting for a change of horses on a coach bound for Belfast, and returned to the care of her mother who expressed her sincere gratitude to the gentleman for the rescue of her daughter, and then departed for home all the while vascillating between expressing feelings of joy at being reunited with her daughter, and remonstrating her for allowing romantic fantasies to overrule good judgement and risk the reputation of her family.

Sir Thomas and Lady Bertram were preparing to depart as well. After he and Viscount Dalrymple returned from scouring Dublin for the missing girl and left the search in the hands of Colonel Fitzwilliam's agents, they made their way back to Rathclare Hall to await word, which arrived the next day and confirmed Mary was safely in hand and enroute by way of a hired carriage. Once she and Colonel Fitzwilliam arrived and after learning some of the details of the rescue, they prepared to begin their journey home to Mansfield Park.

"One cannot always depend on the good judgement of their children nor keep them out of the reach of unworthy, cunning men," declared Sir Thomas. "That Miss Jameson has been returned safely and unharmed is due to the quick thinking and action on the part of Colonel Fitzwilliam. I am proud to have contributed by participating in the search and grateful for a happy outcome."

"Indeed, my dear husband, what you did was most heroic and praiseworthy," replied Lady Bertram. "Your family will hear of your actions and may it serve as a reminder to them of the importance of adhering to proper social conduct as is expected of a family of rank and importance. I, for one, will sing your praises."

Following the departure of Mrs. Jameson with her daughter, and the Bertrams, the immediate family was eager to hear every point about the pursuit, the villain's scheme, and how the colonel managed to extract Mary from the control of the infamous Duncan Woulff.

"I rode hard the first hours knowing they would be travelling more slowly in the gig and would have to refresh the horse or switch to a public coach. I followed the coaching route and came upon them at an inn early that evening. She was alone at a dining table when I walked in and her countenance registered my identity immediately, for she blushed and turned away.

"I begged leave to join her and within a few minutes,

Woulff arrived having arranged a room for the night so they could rest until the coach departed early in the morning. His expression upon seeing me turned dark and he affected an arrogant pose of self-rightousness, as though he was the young lady's protector and I the philanderer. He challenged me by what right I had to claim a connection with Miss Jameson and I answered that I was there to claim the girl on behalf of her family from whom she had been snatched away, by someone wholly unconnected to them, with no rights or privileges associated with her care.

"'She is here of her own free will and we are engaged to marry at the soonest possible time,' he replied.

"I demanded to know, 'If you are truly engaged, then why is she not with her family planning for the nuptials? By what right do you run off with an innocent young lady leaving her without the protection of her family? I am here on their behalf while others search for you in Dublin lest you attempt to abduct her by sea. I insist you turn her over to my care this very moment and I will see her safely returned to her mother, who is desperate with worry'.

"'You have no more claim on her than I do, sir. Leave us be and go about your business,' he answered.

"'Miss Mary Jameson is my business. Yours is to attach yourself to someone of wealth and consequence to enrich yourself at her expense by way of elopement. If we are to talk business, sir, how much will it take for you to release her to my care in lieu of attempting to take over her inheritance through marriage?'

"Miss Jameson sat in stunned silence at this exchange and

finally meekly spoke up and said, 'Please, Colonel Fitzwilliam, Duncan loves me and I love him'.

"'I fully comprehend the situation', I answered, 'although I am not convinced you do, Miss. This man standing before you is a fortune hunter who has taken advantage of your affection by pretending to return that love. He has a history of callously seducing young ladies, putting them in the family way, and then abandoning them. He only wishes to marry you for your inheritance'. Then, turning to Woulff, I demanded that he name his price.

"'I am not so easily bought, sir', he replied but he recognised my resolve.

"'I have a banking relationship in Ireland and can arrange a transfer of funds to you tomorrow. Name your price to leave this innocent young lady alone, and be on your way. What say you?'

"He avoided looking her in the eyes but managed to mutter two thousand pounds. I countered with one thousand pounds with the promise not to report him to the authorities, and to this he finally agreed. The poor lady was shocked and devasted at the outcome but I escorted her to the room that had been arranged and insisted he find other accomodations while I guarded her door for the night. The next day I visited a bank, transferred the funds, and arranged to hire a private carriage by which we made our way here."

"We are greatly in your debt, sir," said the viscount. "A repayment for your generosity will be arranged immediately, but truly, sir, we can never repay you for the acumen of your plan and your own swift action to save our family's reputation."

His mother, the dowager, added, "This is what happens when young ladies are taught foreign languages and foreign ways; these things go to their heads and inflame their passions. Too much education in a woman can be very bad indeed."

His wife, Augusta, replied, "To be sure there will be no more Italian spoken in this household and I shall burn all the masks from the ball as well."

Later that day at Rathclare Park, Catherine and Edward walked in the garden. "Poor Mary must have been devastated by the scene you described; abandoned by the man she adored whom she thought loved her for the price of a thousand pounds. She was so hopelessly romantic that I am sure she must have cried all the way home in the carriage."

"Indeed, she was overcome with anguish and I gave her privacy by riding behind the carriage. When we stopped at a changing station and we went inside to get some refreshment, I shared a story of my own experience that helped to soothe her."

"Would it be importune of me to ask what the story was?" asked Catherine.

"No, indeed, for you know the person of whom I shall speak, Georgiana Darcy, now Mrs. James Baldwin, and presently residing in Bath."

"To be sure, I am shocked. Who would dare prey on that lovely lady with all her wealth and connections? Unquestionably Mr. Darcy would be a formidable adversary for anyone to risk his wrath by attempting such a thing, or yours, for that matter, as her other guardian. How is it possible?"

"Mr. Wickham was the son of the estate manager for Mr. Darcy's father and they grew up together as boys on the family estate, Pemberley. The elder Mr. Darcy was very fond of his god-son and liberally bestowed opportunities on Wickham, raising him as a gentleman and paying for a Cambridge education in hopes he would choose a profession in the Church, even leaving him a legacy upon his death. Instead, he turned down the living, accepted a three thousand pound settlement from Darcy and went on to lead a reckless life of idleness and dissipation.

"He later returned to ask for additional financial support and was turned away, but rather than accepting the answer, he designed a scheme to renew a relationship with Georgianna, a mere 15 years old at the time, persuaded her of their mutual love, and convinced her to elope with him. Had he succeeded, he would have achieved his first object, access to her fortune of thirty thousand pounds and his second object, the humiliation of Darcy. Fortunately, Darcy discovered them and was able to disrupt the plan, return her to his care, and cast Wickham off forever. When your cousin heard this testament about the deceit of men whom a young lady should be able to trust, it served to provide some solace for her broken heart."

"What a travesty to take advantage of someone as modest and shy as Mrs. Baldwin at such a tender age. May I ask what became of Wickham? Has he remained banished from their lives as he deserved?"

"Ah, that is another story entirely," replied Edward. "Unfortunately he still hovers on the edges of our society even though he went on to demonstrate even worse behaviour by eloping with Mrs. Darcy's youngest sister, Lydia, prior to Elizabeth's marriage to my cousin. Wickham had joined the militia and was stationed near the home of the Bennets who had five daughters. He was a great favourite in the community until the militia moved on to Brighton and he left behind multiple debts and talk of dalliances in his wake. Lydia was engaged to travel to Brighton as the guest of the colonel's wife, and then eloped with Wickham to the dismay and shame of her family. It was only through Darcy's efforts to track them down in London and interceed with Wickham by offering a large sum of money that they were married and the family's reputation was spared."

"As my maid, Birdie, would say, I am gobsmacked."

Edward laughed and replied, "It is a convoluted story but I can assure you that Wickham is forbidden anywhere near Darcy and his family. This is, of course, a very private matter but I could not withhold it from you; I respect you too much, and would rather confide in you than hide the truth."

"You may rely on my confidentiality," Catherine assured him. "The service you did for us is greater than you know. I was informed by Dean Fitzgerald that word had come from Rome implicating Woulff in a scheme to sell forgeries of ancient coins and works of art to wealthy patrons in the local market and is under investigation, so it seems likely he was greatly in need of money. Fortunately, Trinity was not a victim of the deceit, which is a relief, but I have to ask myself if I would have recognised a fake antiquity should he have presented it as genuine? Would I have been so trusting that I could be taken in? Deceit of this type is an abomination to those of us who seek to present the truth that historical objects reveal."

~~*~*

That evening as she lay in bed, Catherine could not stop thinking about Edward and all that had happened since his arrival. Despite her reluctance to receive him and perturbation with her family for assuming courtship was his plan, considering all the men of her acquaintance, she esteemed him more than any other she had ever known. None could compare; he was well-bred and moved with ease in any social setting; he was a ready conversationalist who could talk as agreeably about travelling as staying home and express intelligent opinions on books, art, and music; he was good humoured and his manners were admired by all, but there was so much more. He was adventurous, curious, quick-witted, brave, a man of action. She had never known anyone who could pass through the world so effortlessly and yet be so fair-minded, generous, and tolerant. He had no need for artifice, his character was always open and sincere. If ever she could be tempted to marry, surely this was the man.

Chapter 20

Sitting at the desk in her study, Catherine's eyes followed the tiny rainbows cast by the prism hanging in her window. She had taken to opening the curtains in the morning so it could refract light that danced off the floor and bookcases; a pleasant distraction before turning her attention to the manuscripts on her desk. A knock on the door brought the announcement that Colonel Fitzwilliam was in the drawing room and her mother wished her to join them.

When she entered they were discussing his travel plans and how soon he might depart. Upon seeing her, he stood up and suggested they take a walk in the garden, much to her relief since she did not relish any conversation with him that would include her mother's prying eyes and alert ears. They began their stroll past the greenhouse where she experimented with growing medicinal herbs and followed a path to a more wooded area. They walked silently for a while until, at last, he spoke.

"I will be departing soon to return to England and my father's estate, after which I will make my annual visit to Rosings Park to call on my aunt, Lady Catherine. I am loathe to leave Dublin for one reason alone, that I shall no longer have the pleasure of your company, something that I have come to treasure ever since we first met in Bath and I followed you here, for follow you I did. You alone have captured my imagination and justified my aspiration of finding a companion who would meet me on equal terms, whose mind would challenge mine, whose candour would encourage honest communication, whose respect, and dare I say it, love, would fulfill my every hope and dream.

"I know you have never sought my attention, that you are committed to your work, your studies, that your passions have been inflamed by learning and accomplishment; yet I can think of nothing that would give me greater pleasure than lifting you out of your present situation and travelling with you to explore all the subjects that fascinate and excite you. We could visit the continent, Rome and Athens, Egypt even, the ancient places that have so captivated your imagination and scholarly pursuits.

"You told me when we first met that you never intended to marry because you could not accept the concept of being the possession of your husband. I could never think of you as a possession; I subscribe to the old Irish Brehan Laws that regard women as having equal status to men. I realise that society and the laws that exist today do not support the notion, but in my heart that is all that I want in a wife, an equal companion in heart and mind. Surely you must know how much I admire you, love you, long to be with you. I beg you to consider my offer."

Catherine was speechless. She surmised that he had formed an attachment and followed her to Ireland with courtship in mind, just as her family had suspected and eagerly embraced, but she was not prepared to hear the words nor formulate a response. She had spent the night before musing about all the wonderful qualities this person embodied and knew that if she ever was disposed to marry, this would be the man. She felt panic, dismay, and exhileration all at once. A chance to escape the confines of her narrow existence and see the world; to be accepted as she was rather than forced into a mould defined by others was intoxicating, but she was a woman whose body made its own monthly demands and intimacy produced inevitable outcomes, children with ties that bind. As a woman, she would never be free of these constraints or have the same freedoms that men enjoy, but would be obligated to fulfill the role of wife to the man she loved. There it was, the first time she had allowed the thought to surface in her head, 'the man she loved'.

"I admire you more than any other man of my acquaintance and, admittedly, I have longed for the freedom that men enjoy; to travel, explore, experience all that the world has to offer, but it is not the destiny providence chose for me. I was born with the mental aptitude of a man but inhabit a woman's body which is both my great good fortune and my cross to bear. I cannot envision how this disparity can be equalised just by virtue of agreeing to marry, whatever feelings I may have for you."

"Then you have formed an attachment? Is my fondest hope realised? Is it possible you share my regard? Do not toy with me, Catherine. Are my feelings reciprocated despite your reluctance to claim it?" He reached out and took her hands in his. "Please tell me I may have hope."

It was not within her power to deny and Catherine nodded her assent.

"Marry me, my dearest Catherine? Will you make me the happiest of men and I hope in turn, you the happiest of women? I promise you will not regret it; our life together will be sublime; we will be equals in spirit and in outlook; you need not fear losing yourself to a position of obeisance to your husband. I shall not ask that of you. Say yes, I beg you."

With her heart fluttering in her chest as it never had before, Catherine looked into his eyes and answered, "Yes."

"Oh, my dearest Catherine, I promise you will never regret your decision. Come, let us go immediately to tell you mother."

"Please, wait, for I am quite overcome. You must give me a little time before I face my mother; the news will bring her great joy but I must consider how to share it in my own way. Return tomorrow, dearest Edward, and we shall settle the matter; I need a little time is all."

~~*~*

Catherine sat staring in the mirror after Birdie finished brushing her hair and turning back the bed, her gaze reflecting the apprehension that overwhelmed her. Was this the right decision? Why did she feel anxious rather than elated? Was this the way love was supposed to feel? Everything in her life was suddenly upended and for the first time she knew not what to think. Having always depended on her ability to reason and observe, to rely on her intellect to guide her, and knowing an inheritance from her father allowed her a measure of control over her life, she had settled into a carefully curated independence, aloof from the cares that burdened others of her gender. She was not like other women; those attributes that defined most of the women she knew were entirely missing in her. She had no patience for the banal discussions of the latest fashions, upcoming balls, or neighbourhood gossip that always occurred in the company of women. Her mother had forced her into that world but it was not one she could comfortably inhabit.

Since she reached puberty she realised that she could not fit in nor did she want to belong in a world of women; teasing, flirting, adorning themselves, moulding themselves to attract the attentions of young men who had no more on their minds than bragging about their shooting matches, fox hunts, and female conquests. It was all as foreign to her as her love of Latin and Greek and fascination with history was foreign to them. She did not fit in and became anxious whenever she had to perform in public at social events where she felt constantly scrutinised and inevitably judged, especially by her own mother, who pulled her in one direction while her father pulled her in another. He recognised her unique intelligence and understood her social awkwardness and shyness; he protected her and planned for her future independence. He may have hoped she would some day find an attachment to a suitable man who understood her gifts, but he accepted that may not come to pass.

Aloofness and disdain were the defences she developed to avoid active participation in entertainments where she was forced to mingle, but now, suddenly, she fretted about her social and personal shortcomings, which would be manifestly unbecoming in the wife of the second son of an earl who moved with such ease in society, full of good humour and friendly manners. The tools she had developed as an adolescent would no longer be of use in that new world.

Observing herself in the mirror, she saw an unremarkable face, plain and pale, with fine hair and a thin frame; suddenly she was filled with self-reproach at all of her deficiencies, ones she had long ago dismissed as unimportant. What would his family and friends say about his selection of a wife? Would they scorn her dedication to learning as being of little material value, unbecoming even, as her mother had? Would he come to feel ashamed of her appearance, her social reserve, her innate shyness? What of intimacy? Would she experience normal feelings of attraction and desire after suppressing such thoughts for so long? She had no recollection of physical affection as a child from either parent and whatever curiosity she experienced in her adolescent years about the sensations of holding hands, kissing, being embraced by a boy, had long since disappeared. A youthful infatuation with her tutor and the warmth of his smile was all she had ever known. When she finally came to understand the process of procreation from one of her books, the more committed she became to never marrying and the more aloof her demeanour became. She had convinced herself she had no need for it, that such urges were for others to experience, and now she was facing the reality of a man who loves her, a husband, expecting her to fulfill the duties of a wife. What if she was not stirred by affection or able to meet his needs?

The prospect of travelling with Edward was exhilerating in its appeal, but how long would it last? Intimacy with him meant the possibility of creating a family which would curtail their freedom to travel and pull her away from the safety and quiet of her study into a world of managing a household, rearing children, and hosting guests. Who would she be then? Where would they live? Her self esteem was based entirely upon her exceptional abilities as a scholar with a facility for languages and a body of knowledge that was valued by a small circle of admirers at Trinity College. Her life was built around that core of influence and it was all she knew. Who was she without that? Would she lose herself trying to become someone she never aspired to be?

For the first time since the passing of her father, Catherine watched tears roll down her cheeks as her fears preyed on her mind and her insecurities grew, and although she eventually climbed into her bed, she spent an anguished night grappling with her demons. When morning arrived, she sent word she had a headache and had tea and biscuits brought to her room. After dressing, she assigned Birdie to be on watch for the appearance of Colonel Fitzwilliam, and ordered her to direct him to the garden where she would be waiting when he arrived. Birdie looked at her expectantly but was dismissed with a wave.

Chapter 21

Catherine paced up and down in the garden endeavouring to compose herself, racked by apprehension of what was to come, but resolved to face the consequences of a decision she knew would cause pain to someone for whom she cared deeply. When Edward entered the garden his countenance manifested joy that emanated from within but his beaming smile soon gave way on his first glance of her and the smile was dismissed.

"What is the matter, my love, what distresses you?"

Her eyes were cast downwards for she could not meet his gaze. "I find myself unprepared to accept your offer of marriage, Edward, for I cannot find it in myself to embrace such a drastic change in my life. I know your love is sincere, but I am convinced that I would not make you a suitable wife and in the end, I would only disappoint you, and cause you more pain than you may feel at this moment. My love and admiration for you compel me to wish for your happiness above my own, and I cannot envision a world in which I can make you happy as your wife.

"I am an anomaly in this world, an incongruous mixture of intelligence and awkwardness. I do not long for the things most women long for. I do not know how to please others; I've only ever sought to please myself because of my own sense of superiority, misguided though it may be. My manners are not always what they should be; I have not the talent for conversation that so many have; I never bothered to learn how to appear interested in the concerns of others. By valuing my own abilities above all things, I have succumbed to pride to the degree that I am unsuitable as a companion. I do not know how to be other than what I am and you deserve so much more; someone who matches your amiability and joyful embrace of the world; someone who understands and feels affection for others; someone you will be proud to escort among your family and friends, whom they can respect and admire. My particular attributes are not much admired in most social circles and you cannot overlook these deficiencies. You must see that?"

"I see nothing of the sort. I have spent enough time in your company to know in my heart that you are the companion of my dreams, my muse. While I rejoice that I have found such a unique treasure, you denigrate yourself to such a degree that you would lock yourself away from future happiness for fear of the opinion of others, fear of intimacy, fear of what the future may bring. I have no wish to change you, to turn you into a different creature than you are today. If you love me, affection will follow even if you've never contemplated it before. If we have children, they need not keep us from exploration and adventure even if they temporarily delay it. Did Grace O'Malley's motherhood deter her ambition? She gave birth to her son on a ship and then went on deck to battle pirates, and but for that event, she never would have met the Queen of England to negotiate for the release of that same son, which served to launch the success of her family for generations to come. Will you let fear govern your decisions? Your sense of adventure? Where is your courage?"

"Even now I fail you, for I cannot deny what you say, I admit that I lack courage. I have been too long used to the order of my life, sheltered as it is, and nothing will induce me to change. I do not know how to inhabit the world you live in. I will not measure up. I will disappoint you. You must let go of me and trust that you will find your way to a companion who will truly make you happy. Please accept my decision."

The crestfallen look of disappoinment on Edward's face was evidence enough of his decimated hopes. Finally he said, "I shall not take leave of your mother. Please give her my regards. I shall importune you no longer. Farewell."

When Catherine reentered the house her mother was eagerly waiting for her and immediately took note of her downcast look.

"Where is Colonel Fitzwilliam? Has he left without saying goodbye?"

"He sends his regards but was in a hurry to be off. He travels tomorrow to England."

"Is this how it is to end?" demanded her mother. "Have you managed to discourage yet another suitor? One who was clearly enamoured with you though why, I shall never understand. You certainly gave him no encouragement. How could you? Foolish girl! Will you lock yourself in your darkened study and hide away from the rest of the world forevermore? Someday I will be gone, and so will your father's old friends at the college, and you will be a lonely old spinster whom no one shall seek out, not even for your precious opinions. You will be passed by. Irrelevant. You have thrown away a chance at true happiness with a man who clearly loved and admired you. You could have had a life, a real life in the real world, instead of hiding away in the confines of your dusty old study. Foolish, foolish girl."

Catherine retreated to her room and declined to dine with her mother. Even Birdie was dismissed from her duties as she sank into a despondency that she had never felt before. Was her mother right? Had she defined her own destiny to live alone in the world where all her gifts and knowledge would be dismissed and forgotten? Was fear triumphing over future happiness with a companion who loved and valued her as no one else had in her life. Had vanity and pride been her folly? Would avoiding the world instead of living in the world be her undoing? Her entire life was suddenly upended and she was unmoored from all of the landmarks that had anchored her. She spent another sleepless night and arose very early in the morning to go to her study where she opened the curtain, removed the prism that hung there, wrapped it carefully, and placed it in her desk drawer next to the small box containing the antique silver button, the remnant of a long ago love affair and poignant symbol of a rejected lover.

Later that morning there was a knock on the door. It was her mother, who rarely if ever crossed the threshold of her study, silently delivering an unopened letter addressed to her from Colonel Fitzwilliam.

Dearest Catherine,

You have given me no choice but to move forward with my life even if it means leaving my heart behind. I shall not admonish you; it was I who chose to risk it. You were always open and sincere about your intentions so I cannot fault you, but I was so captivated from the start by your intelligence and wit that I convinced myself I could win your heart. I believe that I succeeded despite your resistance, since you claim that you declined my proposal because of your deep affection and wishes for my happiness. I never imagined fear of failure would guide your decision and I truly believe it is at the cost of your own happiness and you will come to regret it, for once you have opened your heart it is difficult to lock it away again.

I wish you had the courage to trust in a future with me for I know that you can be brave. I shall never forget your audaciousness in convincing me to take you to that pub and your spirited recitation of an Irish blessing, with your colour high, your voice clear and resonant; you never were more beautiful than on that day.

I shall importune you no longer other than to say I believe you have made a mistake that hurts us both deeply and you will come to regret. May I suggest you write a note to enclose with Grace O'Malley's silver button gifted to you by the Marquess of Sligo that reads, "The heart of Edward Fitzwilliam", for it shall always be yours.

With great respect and true affection,

EF

Tears welled in her eyes and made a hot path down her cheeks as she carefully folded the letter and placed it in the drawer with the prism and the button. Never had she questioned her own judgement so acutely or felt the impact of a decision so deeply. Emotion was not a companion she was used to encountering; on the contrary, she had carefully managed her life so as to avoid such feelings and the confrontation with these new sensations caused her to withdraw from everyone.

She found no enthusiasm for her usual routines, reading, examining, analysing, or writing. When she tried to will herself back into those familiar patterns they seemed empty and irrelevant. She avoided almost everyone, self consciously aware that her family judged her more harshly than usual, perceiving her as a failure in ways different than before. Her independence was now pitied rather than tolerated for it had never been admired. She was allowed to withdraw socially because it was part of her pattern of avoidance anyway and was expected. To escape the confines of her study she spent time in her personal garden but found little to comfort her there. One day she brought the prism to hang in the greenhouse but the colourful refractions did more to disturb her spirits than comfort them so she returned it to the desk drawer. She had forsaken colour and light in her life.

A few weeks after Edward's departure she forced herself to visit Dean Fitzgerald at Trinity to return some books and make her excuses for falling behind on a project. His look of disappointment on learning that Colonel Fitzwilliam was gone with no plan of returning was followed with benevolent solicitousness that only served to increase her discomfort.

"I'm sorry to hear he has gone, my dear Catherine. He was a fine man who greatly admired you and particularly respected your dedication to learning. I hope your voracious appetite for knowledge provides a salve for losing such a noble friend. I understand that your projects have fallen behind, but please do not worry as it may take time for you to regain enthusiasm for your studies."

"I have been importuned by all of the distractions of the past few months from the arrival of Colonel Fitzwilliam to the betrayal by Duncan Woulff. I cannot deny the attachment he felt for me but I believe such a fine man is deserving of an amiable wife and I have not the capacity to become that person. I assure you of my readiness to continue my efforts to contribute to the body of knowledge so important to this department. It is my life's work."

"Ah, yes. Your contributions are highly valued and respected here at Trinity, but, my dear, there is more to life than the study of antiquities and ancient languages. You are still young. I do hope you don't sacrifice your personal happiness for the work of this institution when there are wonders to discover outside these walls and those of your study," he said kindly.

It seemed everyone she knew saw her circumstances as a

self-inflicted misfortune due to her conceited independence and stubborn adherence to intellectual pursuits over the benefits of a meaningful, loving attachment to someone who cared for her deeply, and from these opinons there was no escape.

Chapter 22

Sometime thereafter Margaret Jameson and her daughter, Mary, came to call on their way to visit Charles and Augusta for a week. It would be the first time Mary had seen them since her flight from home with Duncan Woulff and eventual recovery by Colonel Fitzwilliam. Mary cautiously knocked on the door of her study and gained admittance.

"How well you look, Mary. I'm glad to see you recovered from your ordeal. Won't you take a seat?"

"Thank you, Catherine. I am grateful my visage does not betray the emotions I still struggle to conceal for Mamma's sake. I believe it will take time for a full recovery from my foolish venture. I feel so betrayed and ridiculous based on my own reckless imprudence, but I suppose time will heal my wounds, or so Mamma tells me. She has been good enough to forgive my dalliance and blame it on youthful inexperience for which I am grateful; moreover, she blames herself as much as anyone for we all succumbed to such extravagant admiration of Mr. Woulff's person and address that no one perceived his alterior motives and deceptions." She gave a small sad sigh and continued.

"I'm told Colonel Fitzwilliam has returned to England and I am sorry that I did not get a chance to say goodbye or properly thank him. He is such a fine man, brave and honourable; I do so admire him."

"Yes," replied Catherine. "He did the family a great service for which we are all grateful."

"He was so kind to me and showed such forebearance that I shall never forget him. When we started out, I was giddy with excitement for the adventure and enthralled with Mr. Woulff, whom I truly believed loved me and that we were meant to be together. To be honest, I was out of my senses for him, yet when we stopped that night and I was sitting alone in the way station sipping tea and awaiting accomodations for the night, I began to have doubts and was filled with self reproach for my headstrong decision, knowing it was too late. The die had been cast. When I saw Colonel Fitzwilliam approach, my heart jumped in my throat and I trembled with anxiety mixed with relief thinking there might be a way out. When he confronted Mr. Woulff, I realised immediately that the man I had intended to marry had neither integrity nor honour and my good opinion of him was completely overthrown. The invectives they exchanged made me realise that I was just a pawn, a means to an end, and when an amount was settled upon to pay off that scoundrel of a man to relinquish me, I was so disheartened and ashamed. I can assure you I cried that night like never before but felt relieved and comforted that Colonel Fitzwilliam was there to protect me.

"The next day, after the transaction was completed, Colonel Fitzwilliam arranged a private carriage for me but refused to ride alone with me for propriety's sake so he rode on horseback. It was just as well for I spent most of the time sobbing wretchedly and berating myself for all I had put my family through. I was so miserable and chastened I could not bear to face anyone. When we stopped at a changing station, he joined me while we waited. I'm sure my eyes were red and swollen from crying but he showed such sympathy for my pitiable state and he gently took my hand in his and asked permission to tell me a story of a young lady who, much like me, had been betrayed by someone she should have been able to trust.

"Did you know he has a young cousin, recently married, who was taken advantage of when she was just my age by someone with whom she had been raised? He was the son of the estate manager who was raised like a son alongside the young lady and her older brother who was to inherit the family estate. He turned out to be wild, a gambler and carouser; he squandered the inheritance he received and came back asking for more. By then the estate had passed into the hands of Colonel Fitzwilliam's cousin and they both had been tasked with overseeing the upbringing of the young lady, Georgianna by name. When the entreaty for more money was refused, the scoundrel conceived a new plot to seduce Georgianna and convince her to elope with him.

"Imagine my shock hearing this story so much like my

own! Luckily, her brother discovered the plot and was able to intercede before it was too late, just as Colonel Fitzwilliam did for me."

"Colonel Fitzwilliam shared this story with me as well," replied Catherine. "Clearly men who lack character and use their arts to captivate innocent young ladies in hopes of making their fortune have no shame."

"His story brought me such comfort, I can assure you, and made the rest of my journey more tranquil while I gathered myself to face the consequences of my behaviour and confront the censure of my family. He is everything a gentleman ought to be, open and honest, kind and reassuring, yet strong and resourceful. The way he handled Mr. Woulff with such confidence and authority was something to behold. And he is so fond of you, Catherine. He spoke of you with such admiration and I was so hoping that you would find it in your heart to accept him. You could not find a better man in all the world and I was very sorry to hear he had departed alone. I'm sure you must miss his good humour and intelligence, his adventurousness and bravery. I shall never forget the letter he wrote and the gift he presented to you; it was so romantic, the silver button from the pirate queen, but now it is over I suppose, and we are both alone with our thoughts and regrets."

Catherine tried to assure her that while she greatly admired Colonel Fitzwilliam she had no regrets, but her protestation felt hollow even to herself. Still, she was grateful Mary understood what a narrow escape she made from an imprudent elopement as it would make her more cautious in the future. It further elevated Edward as well, as a quick witted man of action who had saved her family from a scandal at the hands of an adverturous rogue, and they would always be in his debt. After Mary and her mother departed, she found herself more despondent than ever and grappled with the seemingly impossible task of freeing her mind from the thoughts that so vexed her.

Where was he now? Was he still visiting his aunt and cousin? Was he beseiged on all sides by pressure to make an alliance for the sake of the family fortune? Did he bristle at the constraints of society's imperative for a second son to marry well? Was his pedantic aunt haranguing him to make a decision and marry his cousin? At other times she imagined that he met a lively, intelligent woman with beauty, grace, and good humour. Someone witty like Mrs. Darcy, whom she knew to be a favourite of his. That was the outcome she hoped for most, to assuage her own guilt for rejecting his proposal.

Yes, of course, there was a comely young lady with all the proper social graces who would come into his life and help mend his broken heart. She would lift his spirits, soothe his feelings of loss and frustration, provide the unguent he needed so he could move on with his life, be happily married, and raise lively, robust children with a wife who worshipped him. Yes, of course, that was bound to happen. He would put his feelings for her behind him and move on to a rewarding, loving relationship with someone else, someone worthy. He would forget her and Dublin and his journey and the pirate queen and the silver button; they would be left behind, a distant memory of a long ago adventure. Of this she was sure, except when she was not, and her mind wandered back to entrapment in a loveless marriage with a domineering mother-in-law overseeing his life and that of her daughter. Every day, it was the same vascillation of thoughts repeating the stories she told herself. The one caused her to feel guilt that she could have made him happy, the other soothed her conscience as she assured herself she had made the right decision to refuse him; that it had been for his own happiness and fulfillment, that in the end he would be grateful, of that she was sure.

Chapter 23

"It seems we shall be celebrating an anniversary in Bath this season, Catherine. I've just received a letter from Lady Elizabeth Bertram and they plan to return there in honour of their first anniversary. We shall have to plan an event to help them celebrate, perhaps not the large reception we hosted last year; something more intimate, I think. Certainly it will include the Wentworths and Musgroves as they are relations, and Lady Russell, of course. Since we were invited to the engagement party for Dr. Baldwin and Miss Darcy who have since married, it would be appropriate to invite them as well; and her brother, Mr. Darcy, and his charming wife are just the right sort of people to include. I shall encourage Augusta and Charles to make a sojourn to Bath as they are quite fond of Sir Thomas and Elizabeth, having hosted them so recently in Dublin. I've already begun arrangements for our stay at the Royal Crescent and will expand it to include them."

"Must we go to Bath again, Mamma? Surely we have exhausted the possibilities for entertainment there, and we have recently seen the Bertrams. It seems like an excessive exertion of effort after all the time we have spent with them of late. After all, their visit here was an extended trip to celebrate their marriage as it is, so how much more celebrating can be necessary?" replied Catherine.

"I am determined we shall go to Bath despite your protestations, Catherine. You need not worry about being invited to dance by a gentleman of rank or endeavours towards courtship any longer. You have dismissed that opportunity decisively enough and, besides, I should like to see Dr. Baldwin again. I find myself suffering from pains and spasms almost daily and wish to consult with the doctor and, perhaps, experience the treatments he devises for his patients. He is a prominent physician with a highly regarded reputation in the community, and why should I not try his remedies just as our cousin, Sir Walter Elliot did?"

"Sir Walter died of a stroke, Mamma."

"That does not mean he did not benefit from the treatments prior to his death and a friend of Lady Russell's has been helped immensely by his ministrations. Would you have me suffer when there is the potential of my finding relief in the mineral waters of Bath? Have you no compassion for my delicate condition, for my pain and suffering?

"I know how your mind operates. You are hoping to avoid contact with friends and relatives of Colonel Fitzwilliam but I will not allow you to abandon new acquaintances just because of your own foolish decision to reject an offer of marriage from such a worthy gentleman. You cannot hide away from the world and I shall not be held back by your desire to avoid society here or in Bath. I insist we travel there for the Season and you shall have to make the best of it. Besides, you always enjoy wandering the excavation site of the Roman baths and mingling amongst the labourers in the dirt and dust while aprising the remnants of ancient history they uncover. Surely that will keep you occupied."

It was true, of course. One of the attractions for Catherine was her acceptance by the excavators of the ancient ruins and ability to get a first hand view of their discoveries. Her input was invaluable as there was no one else as well versed in Roman history with the ability to identify images and translate the Latin phrases they might uncover. She was always comfortable in that setting and could think of no other response than, "As you wish, Mamma."

~~*~*

Augusta and Charles were enthralled with the plan to visit Bath as they had never been and were equally eager to renew their friendship with Sir Thomas and Lady Bertram. There was much to discuss since the departure of the newlyweds to their estate at Mansfield Park. The scandal around the elopement of young Mary Jameson had been deftly concealed before word had time to spread among their acquaintances. Colonel Fitzwilliam's quick action to apprehend the scoundrel and retrieve the young lady had dampened any gossip from spreading. The handsome tutor who attracted so much admiration and attention was summarily dismissed along with any references to the Italian language that had been so eagerly adopted when he first arrived. They were ready for new distractions and to make new acquaintances of the right sort.

There was nothing for Catherine to do but submit to the plans and gird herself to deal with the anxiety she knew she would experience as she faced the judgement sure to be rendered by all as the foolish, independent woman who made the unpropitous decision to choose a solitary life for the useless pursuit of knowledge and expertise, over a tender attachment to an amiable man of distinction who clearly admired her despite her plain appearance and diffident nature.

There would be no avoiding Dr. Baldwin and his wife, Georgianna, and, by extension, Mr. and Mrs. Darcy if they returned for the Season. She wondered if they had seen Edward and were aware she backed out of an engagement that she had agreed to after one night, although surely they would know his whereabouts. Was he still visiting his aunt and cousin or had he ventured on to other places? Would he visit Bath again this year? Had he shared his disappointment over her refusal to marry him? Had he revealed news of his adventure travelling to Waterford and on to Connacht in search of evidence of a pirate queen and returned with a gift for her? She endeavoured to manage the apprehension that vexed her on a daily basis and only increased as the departure approached, but it was difficult to quell the unease. Even her family sensed it. They eagerly discussed plans for the trip but quieted when she was within hearing distance, not out of pity or sensitivity for her feelings, but because her presence acted as a suppressant to their enthusiasm.

"We must make sure there is an announcement in the society column of the Bath newspaper about our arrival in town as well as to cover the details of the anniversary party for the Bertrams," declared Augusta. "I am sure our appearance on the scene will draw attention from all the right sorts who will be eager to make our acquaintance, so I shall have to shop for new gowns for the occasion. I'm sure Lady Bertram will be the height of fashion in any ensemble she chooses to wear and I shall not be outdone by her if I can help it. Don't you agree, Charles?"

"Whatever you wish, my dear," he replied. "And what of the children? Shall we plan to bring them?"

"Oh dear me, no! We should have to hire an extra carriage for them and their nanny and extra rooms at the Royal Crescent when they would be perfectly cared for here at home. There is no need to bring the children. After all, we will only be gone a short time and their comfort is my first concern, as always. We need have no concern on that front."

"I do hope our new acquaintances include sporting men who enjoy outdoor activities such as riding and shooting," said Charles. "I must have some entertainment outside of dinner parties, promenades, musical concerts, and balls."

"Have no fear on that front, Charles," replied his mother. "Mr. Thomas Baldwin, the heir to the Baldwin estate, shares your tastes and interests. He is known to be a sportsman and we shall have contact with the family early on since I intend to seek out the services of his brother, Dr. Baldwin, and enjoy the restorative benefits of the mineral baths while I'm there. I am told the entire experience can be transformative and, at my age, I am in need of healing and comfort. I understand he uses a bathing chair to immerse you in the water which sounds exhilerating."

Chapter 24

The arrival of Catherine and her mother was duly noted in the society column of the local Bath newspaper as expected and they settled into their apartments to begin planning the celebration of the one year wedding anniversary of Sir Thomas Bertram to their cousin, the former Elizabeth Elliot. With the date fixed, correspondence was exchanged to determine the scheduled arrivals in Bath of Elizabeth's family, specifically, Captain Wentworth and his wife, Anne, as well as Charles Musgrove and his wife, Mary, and his parents, Mr. and Mrs. Musgrove. The extended guest list included Lady Russell, a long time friend of the Elliot family, Dr. James Baldwin and his wife, Georgianna, and Mr. Thomas Baldwin with his wife, Kitty. It was hoped that Mr. and Mrs. Darcy from the great estate of Pemberley would also be in town in time for the celebration. Although Colonel Fitzwilliam stood as best man for Sir Thomas during the wedding, no one had any idea of his plans or whether he would visit Bath this Season at all.

They held off on social engagements awaiting the arrival of Charles and Augusta, whom the dowager knew would be eager to embrace any and all the entertainments available. Catherine was assigned to hand deliver a few local invitations as part of her mother's effort to force her out into the social milieu despite knowing her reluctance; she was determined to not allow her daughter to hide away as she had been used to for the past few months at home where she had even curtailed her visits to Trinity College. Late one morning, Catherine found herself calling on Lady Russell at her current residence of Laurel Place to deliver the invitation.

"Miss Carteret, I am delighted to see you. I read in the newspaper that you and your mother had arrived in town for the Season and are soon to be followed by your brother, the viscount, and his wife. It is ever so gracious of you to take the time to deliver the invitation for the anniversary celebration of dear Elizabeth and Sir Thomas; how can it possibly be almost a year gone by since we attended their wedding? What a whirlwind their courtship was, only a month or so, but where love is concerned, time is of no importance when two hearts come together and beat as one, would you agree?

"I understand they visited you recently in Dublin and were hosted by your brother and his wife at their estate. How enchanting, and Lady Bertram had nothing but accolades to share about their visit to your country and the amiable time they spent at Rathclare Hall. She sang the praises of the viscountess as a most charming hostess who planned many entertainments for them, and she also spoke of the cordial treatment by your mother as well. How wonderful to see family bonds grow and flourish despite the loss of my dear friend, the late, lamented Sir Walter Elliott. How good of Viscount Dalrymple and his wife to travel all this way for the anniversary party; I am ever so eager to meet them. I could not be more delighted to receive your invitation and thank you for delivering it in person rather than sending it by messenger. It is so very gracious of you. The Season in Bath is off to a rapturous start already and we will soon be joined by Elizabeth's sisters and their husbands, the Wenthworths and the Musgroves, which will make for a most delightful reunion."

Catherine did her best to appear engaged and pleasant although she would rather have been anywhere, doing anything, than trapped in a discussion about one of the people she least admired in the world, her cousin, Elizabeth and her egotistical husband. She had been so grateful the newlyweds were hosted by her brother and Augusta when they arrived in Dublin, for though she had been forced into many unwelcome social occasions during their stay, at least she did not have to encounter them on a daily basis had they stayed at Rathclare Park, and they travelled north to purchase linens and lace which provided another reprieve. Everything about this conversation reminded her of Edward, the memory of whom still weighed heavily on her heart, and whom she knew would be the subject of countless, unavoidable conversations in which she would rather not engage. She extricated herself as quickly as she could and set upon the route to their lodgings realising she could only manage one of these encounters at a time. Since her mother was scheduled to begin her treatments with Dr. Baldwin in a few days, that invitation could be delivered later.

As she turned the corner she found herself face to face with Dr. Baldwin's wife, Georgianna, a most surprising encounter that left her startled and tongue tied. Fortunately, Mrs. Baldwin was gracious and amiable, expressing delight at encountering her so unexpectedly. Gone was the shy young woman she met the previous year with her downcast eyes and soft speaking voice, instead replaced by a confident, self-assured lady eager to greet her and welcome her back to the city she now called home. The transformation was profound and completely unanticipated as she readily engaged in conversation, asking about their trip, their accomodations, their plans, and expressing enthusiasm for the opportunity to renew their friendship.

"I will be delivering an invitation to you to an anniversary party for Sir Thomas and Lady Bertram and we are also wondering if you are expecting your brother, Mr. Darcy and his wife to arrive in Bath any time soon? We are hoping to invite them as well," said Catherine and feeling she must add something to the conversation continued, "I do hope Mrs. Darcy is well as I remember she was in the early stages of pregnancy when last we saw her."

"Oh, they are doing wonderfully well," enthused Georgianna. "Their little boy was born a few months after my wedding and they are rapturously happy. We're expecting them to arrive next week and I know they will be delighted to receive your invitation."

"And your cousin, Colonel Fitzwilliam? Is he expected in

town?" she asked while trying to sound casual. "I remember he stood up as best man for Sir Thomas and I am sure they would welcome his presence at the festivities. He called on us during a trip to Ireland recently while the Bertrams were also in town. Such a small world, is it not?"

"I hope my brother will have word on his whereabouts. I understand he has been enjoying an extended stay at Rosings with our aunt, Lady Catherine, and her daughter, Anne. He always visits annually but this time it appears he has stayed longer than usual. I will certainly let you know if he intends to visit Bath and can partake in the celebration as soon as I receive any report.

"I do hope you will come to call on me at Camden Place which is where we now reside. I remember hearing that you have studied history and science and I have a burgeoning interest in the sciences myself since my marriage to Dr. Baldwin. He has long been committed to research and I am blessed to have an opportunity to support his efforts by aiding him in his studies as well as managing a garden for herbal medicines. We have microscopes in the laboratory that are quite useful for viewing living organisms and plants. I find it fascinating and if you are interested, I would be delighted if you would visit and I could show you our garden and laboratory."

"I can think of nothing I would enjoy more," replied Catherine enthusiastically. "We are just settling in but I shall send a note in the next few days and come to call for I would be eager to view objects through a microscope. How very enticing. I frequently visit friends at Trinity College but have never been offered such an opportunity. Thank you for the kind invitation."

When they parted, Catherine marvelled at the transformation of Georgianna Baldwin and the impact the opportunity for learning could have on a woman. Certainly she was never raised to do anything more than manage the setting of a fine table and raising a fine family and now she was also a valued partner to her husband, helping him with his work and seeming to thrive on the stimulation. What a pity more women were not given the opportunity for an education and to develop their interests.

She then found herself consumed with thoughts of Edward. The news that he remained at Rosings with his aunt and cousin was exactly what she hoped not to hear. She knew the pressure he was under by the family to marry and he was the primary candidate to enter an engagement with his cousin. Her worst fears for his future happiness were made manifest and she was plagued by thoughts of his demanding, shrewish aunt and dreary, sickly cousin pulling him into their orbit.

Chapter 25

Augusta arrived in Bath with a flourish and a voracious appetite to experience all facets of the charming city from promenading around the Pump Room and tasting the waters, to dancing and socialising in the Upper and Lower Assembly rooms, to shopping on Milford Street at the best millineries and dressmakers, to enjoying theatre outings and concerts; she was determined to take it all in and be recognised as a luminary in the social constellation of seasonal arrivals. Her name appeared in the local society column daily and when Sir Thomas and Elizabeth arrived coverage of the socialites was further amplified. They were seen everywhere and their appearance was duly noted to the readers who might aspire to be associated with them. Elizabeth had been used to the attention before the passing of her father, and the resurgence of interest in her comings and goings with the viscountess was particularly gratifying.

For Catherine, the attention focused on her cousin and

sister-in-law allowed her to recede as much as possible from the glare of attention and the relentless activity to pursue her own interests. It was only at small family gatherings that she experienced the brunt of their displeasure with her current status as a single woman who had thrown away a singular opportunity to marry, by dismissing the attentions of an esteemed gentleman of rank who had travelled all the way to Dublin to court her. It was a most egregious decision in the opinion of her extended family.

"I shall never comprehend how a single woman of independent fortune and an elevated status in society, although little to offer by way of appearance, refinement, or fashion to recommend her, would reject the attentions of the son of an earl who clearly admired her and travelled all the way from England with an obvious desire to court her. An unattached woman of mature age and good sense should never reject such an opportunity," commented Elizabeth to Augusta while Catherine sat in the next room in earshot of the conversation. "Surely she cannot intend to stay single all of her life while she pursues recognition of her intellect just because she speaks a few languages and has an interest in antiquities. It is vanity itself and utterly self indulgent, I say, and where is her duty to her family to increase their status and connections? It is unseemly. I was quite shocked to receive your letter apprising me of the situation, Augusta, for she will never receive such an offer again."

"We were all astonishment at the turn of events after what Colonel Fitzwilliam did for her," replied Augusta. "He travelled halfway around Ireland in pursuit of a pointless story about a pirate queen who lived two centuries ago and even brought back a gift for her from a descendant; he rushed into action to apprehend that dissolute Italian tutor and prevent an elopement with our young, naive cousin that would have brought dishonour and shame on the entire family; and most improbably, he seemed to genuinely care for her despite the lack of encouragement on her part. It was a most disappointing outcome I assure you and now she mopes about and hides away in her study and barely speaks to anyone. What could she have been thinking? I shall never understand it."

"Well, I suppose it could be worse. My poor husband is caught in a financial trap supporting his oldest daughter, Maria, who left her husband to pursue her paramour only to end up abandoned, divorced, and penniless. Now we must bear the brunt of the expenses required for her upkeep and that of the aunt who chaperones her. At least your sister-in-law has independent means and isn't a drain on the family. Which is worse, I wonder, succumbing to passion which leads to scorn, isolation, and financial dependency or giving way to an inflated sense of superiority that leads to an empty, loveless existence that no one admires or values? Such folly."

Being the subject of conversations such as this importuned her more deeply than usual; she had been used to such criticism throughout her life but her own emotional turmoil at this time was an affliction only exacerbated by such intrusive commentary. With few places to isolate herself, Catherine spent time visiting the excavation site where daily progress was made uncovering the engineering marvel the Romans had built and the unique artistry it represented depicting mythological tales. The workers had grown used to her visits and supervisors welcomed her observations that could be documented and shared. Anything was better than being dragged along to the Pump Room in the afternoon or to endless teas. Her mother began her sessions with Dr. Baldwin and was enthusiastic about the benefits of his ministrations and Catherine had to admit her complexion was brighter, she had fewer complaints about aches and pains, and seemed to be sleeping better which improved her often dour mood. Now that her mother's schedule was established, Catherine sent a note to Georgianna Baldwin announcing that she would like to visit the garden and laboratory. She was eager for a diversion and enjoyed the company of the young woman with her newly found interest in scientific study; a rarity to find among her female acquaintances.

Her arrival was announced and she was escorted into the drawing room where she was greeted enthusiastically by Georgianna who ordered tea and invited her to sit. "I am so glad you came to call. I have to admit that I feel a certain kinship with you that is uncommon among my female friends, because you have a reputation for scholarly pursuits which is such a rarity. I was raised with many comforts but little education as it was deemed unneccesary for young ladies. We are taught to cover screens, play an instrument, net purses, dance gracefully, and behave modestly with those few accomplishments. I never thought it should be any other way nor did I expect to discover curiosity about the sciences myself. It was not until the first time I visited my husband's laboratory and examined endlessly fascinating objects under a microscope, that it occurred to me there was more in life to be observed than the latest fashions and new styles of hats. My husband has a passion for scientific discovery and I am the beneficiary because he is enthusiatic about my developing interests and welcomes my participation. It is wonderful to have a sense of purpose beyond the confines of what I was taught. I believe your interests also run contrary to the commonly accepted role in society that has been defined for women, and I am so eager to learn of your experiences and to share mine with you."

The layout of Camden Place had changed considerably since the last time Catherine had been there. The spacious drawing rooms were unchanged but alterations had been made to a lower room next to the kitchen which had been converted into a laboratory that looked out over a kitchen garden and greenhouse. The laboratory was neatly kept with shelves holding tubes, vials, and glass slides for viewing specimens. Bookshelves with books and manuscripts lined the wall and a table in the middle of the room featured a large microscope with a smaller one nearby. Two stools were placed side by side in front of the scientific instrument. The exhuberant hostess gathered some sample slides that she placed for viewing and invited Catherine to sit while she gave instructions on how to view the specimens and explained what they were.

Catherine was full of wonder and amazement as she viewed this microscopic world emerging through the lens. She had many questions and observations that were enthusiastically responded to by Georgianna. Catherine knew a little about the history of the development of the instrument using various shaped lenses and light to reveal living microbes and unique cell structures, but Georgianna was able to answer questions that increased her knowledge and sparked her imagination.

"When I return home, I shall insist on visiting the Sciences department at Trinity College to compare their equipment to yours and endeavour to understand what they are learning about the natural world and how they are documenting their studies. I shall have to lean on my friend in the Antiquities department for an introduction because women are not allowed to study there, but I am sure I will find a way to explore the labs unofficially. How lucky you are to have access on a daily basis," commented Catherine.

"What a pity that women are prevented from learning about science and the natural world if they have an interest," replied Georgianna. "How much more we could contribute to the knowledge of the universe if there were no such barriers."

"I am afraid those impediments have existed for centuries although it was not always the case. During the Islamic Golden Age from 900-1200 BC, knowledge of mathematics, science, and astronomy was transferred to Europeans. Even women could be trained and educated and it was centred at the University of Salerno in Italy. The women were known as Salernitas and were allowed to practice medicine, study the use of anesthetics, and even develop prescriptions based on medicinal herbs such as mandrake root and willow bark."

"However did the Salernitas learn such skills so long ago?" asked Georgianna.

"They were world renowned for using a manuscript called

the Trota, or Practical Medicine According to Trota, and that knowledge was shared with women in medicine throughout Europe. I have been privileged to see fragments of a Trota scriptorum in my studies but none survived intact. Unfortunately, the knowledge came to an untimely end for the most sinister of reasons. By the mid-1400's, much of the knowledge was lost due to accusations of witchcraft directed at women herbalists, mid-wives, and medical practicioners who were all forced into hiding."

"How unjust to make such accusations against innocent women. How is it possible?" asked Georgianna.

"Women were an easy target, especially independent, single women with land and wealth that could be confiscated by the Church. As witch hunts increased throughout Europe, so did the use of torture to identify the supposed offenders. Did you know the first book printed by the Gutenberg Press after the Bible was a torture manual developed by two German priests to extract confessions from innocent women accused of witchcraft? It was called the *Maleus Maleficarum*, or *The Hammer of the Witches*. So much knowledge about women's health and fertility was lost because of those heinous practices and the medical profession was eventually wrestled away from women to be taken over by men and requiring a college education that is denied to women."

The shock on Georgianna's face was followed by a gasp. "I grow medicinal herbs in our garden that my husband uses in his medical practice. How can it be that in relatively recent history, as recently as a hundred years ago or more, I could have been accused of witchcraft and sentenced to torture and death? It is difficult to imagine although I know it to be true, for we have all heard of witch hunts. What an abominable practice. I have never viewed what I do as dangerous but there was a time that it was considered to be so."

"We are lucky to live in the age that we do where more opportunities are opening up for women, but many of their contributions over the centuries have been lost, overlooked, or attributed to a male counterpart. Still, we must not lose hope that times will improve and I consider you to be very lucky to have a husband who encourages you to learn and grow. It is a testament to him as well as to you.

"Will you show me your garden? I keep a small one myself, you know, and dabble in testing the effectiveness of medicinal herbs in teas, ointments, and oils. It is a welcome distraction from sitting in my study and provides occasional benefits to others as well as myself. Perhaps we can learn from each other."

"So long as there is no risk of our being burned as witches, I can think of nothing I would enjoy more than a stroll through the garden and sharing the knowledge we both have gathered," laughed Georgianna. "My husband will be most enthused to know we share similar interests."

Chapter 26

A few days later, Catherine decided to stop by Camden Place to drop off some books on medicinal herbs she came across at a local bookstore and lending library. When she entered the drawing room she was surprised to find Mrs. Darcy sitting there looking as lovely and poised as she remembered. Her initial reaction was embarassment for arriving unexpectedly but, even more so, the self-concious awareness that Mr. Darcy and Colonel Fitzwilliam were cousins and close friends so it was very likely that Edward would have confided in them about his rejected proposal when he returned from Ireland. If anyone knew of his intentions prior to his journey, surely it was Mr. and Mrs. Darcy, since Edward was very fond of both and would have taken them into his confidence. She immediately sought to make excuses and quickly depart but had no choice but to join them when they welcomed her warmly and invited her to stay for tea.

They shared the usual pleasantries about travel, the weather, and the Darcy's happiness at the birth of their new son. Last Season they were the family occupying Camden Place but now that Dr. and Mrs. Baldwin became the permanent residents, Mr. and Mrs. Darcy were staying at a roomier apartment nearby that could accomodate their larger staff and young child. They discussed the upcoming anniversary party for Sir Thomas and Lady Bertram and Catherine promised to arrange to have an the invitation delivered to their current residence. Mrs. Darcy asked whether Lady Bertram's sisters would be in attendance at the festivities and who else was expected; inevitably, the conversation turned to the role Colonel Fitzwilliam played in the Bertram wedding and whether they expected him to be in town for the anniversary.

"We heard from our cousin that he very much enjoyed his recent visit to Ireland, Miss Carteret," ventured Mrs. Darcy. "I understand his trip overlapped with Sir Thomas and Lady Bertram's visit which must have made for a most felicitous reunion. Viscount Dalrymple and his wife were most charming, he reported, and included him in several entertainments when he wasn't on tour, for he is such an adventurer, and always seems to be on the move exploring new environs. He spoke most highly of his travels along the coast from Dublin to the south and then north along rugged western shores which he described as breathtaking."

Catherine's heart sank. Surely they knew all; the purpose of his trip to Waterford and Connacht, the gifts he delivered on his return to Dublin, perhaps even her rejection of his proposal. Would he have shared news of her cousin's failed elopement and rescue from a fortune hunter? Perhaps, although she trusted his discretion and gallantry, he may have shared the story because of the connection to Georgianna's own history, just as he had done so to comfort the runaway, Mary.

She could observe no judgement on either woman's face, only warmth and kindness were revealed on their countenances, although it did nothing to relieve her uneasiness. What must they think of her? That this was even a concern reflected the changes of her own perspective, for she had long ago disregarded the opinions of others as it pertained to her life choices; in fact she prided herself on her disdain. Sitting here with two women whom she admired and respected, whose good opinion she valued, brought the realisation that her insulated world had been cracked open ever so slightly and she found herself exposed to the idea that friendship and the regard of those she greatly esteemed, mattered very much to her.

She could avoid the inquiry no longer. "Have you any idea of Colonel Fitzwilliam's travel plans? My cousin and Sir Thomas wonder if he will be in town for the anniversary since he was an integral member of the wedding party and they wish to extend an invitation to him should he be available." She tried to appear as casual and disinterested as possible although her heart was sitting somewhere higher than usual, in her throat.

The two ladies exchanged concerned glances before Mrs. Darcy finally replied, "We have yet to receive word of his travel plans for he has been enjoying an extended stay with his aunt, Lady Catherine De Bourgh, and her daughter, Anne, leaving us to wonder if it is indicative of a larger scheme; that he may, perhaps, have become engaged to Anne. He has not written for some time and we can think of no other reason for the prolonged visit; his habit has always been to spend a week or two annually at Rosings Park, so this is most unexpected. We, of course, wish only that he be happily matched with someone for whom he has a tender and loving attachment; if he has found that with his cousin then we shall be glad of it and wish them well. Lady Catherine is known to have strong opinions and an implacable nature and we have had little contact with her since our own marriage; she even declined to attend the wedding of Georgianna and Dr. Baldwin, so we are reliant on correspondence from Colonel Fitzwilliam for news from Rosings."

Catherine's heart sank from her throat to her stomach with a dull thud. She smiled weakly and nodded while acknowledging that the invitation would remain open in hopes that he would be able to attend and she would relay the information to her family. She managed to extricate herself from the company with excuses to check on her mother who was receiving treatment at the baths.

"I do hope your mother is benefitting from the care of my husband and his staff. He spoke most enthusiastically about welcoming her as a patient and is making every endeavour to relieve her pain and ensure her comfort and tranquillity," said Georgianna as Catherine stood to leave.

"I am sure she will benefit as did I when I underwent

treatments last year," added Mrs. Darcy. "I am certain our healthy young son is a result of the care I received from Dr. Baldwin."

"While Mamma is well past the stage in life for bearing children," smiled Catherine, "I'm sure she will benefit in many other ways and I've observed improvement already." The two ladies laughed at her comment, wished her well, and expressed the hope of seeing her again soon.

Her spirits were low as she walked towards the baths to retrieve her mother and escort her back to the Royal Crescent. The gentleman she esteemed more than any other, the most amiable, intelligent, adventurous person she had ever encountered, now appeared to be on the one path she most hoped he would avoid, that of becoming engaged to a woman he did not love and capitulating to family pressures to marry. It was the worst possible outcome and she felt directly responsible for it because she refused his proposal and drove him away despite his protestations that she would someday regret her decision. He had been prescient because everything about her life was now in upheaval and she could find no peace or contentment, no escape into her usual comforts of quiet study and contemplation. Everything had lost her interest and seemed unimportant, frivolous even.

Perhaps her cousin, Elizabeth, was right when she spoke of her "inflated sense of superiority that leads to an empty, loveless existence that no one admires or values." Harsh words, indeed, but she had no way to counter them and nothing to lean on to support her depressed spirits and emerging regrets. Everything had turned out badly. Despite her brilliant intellect and stubborn attachment to her own independence, she was on unsure footing and found little to give her comfort now, save one thing; as she walked, her fingers travelled to her chemisette and reached underneath to touch the fine silk ribbon around her neck and feel the weight of the object it held close to her bosom, an antique silver button tucked away so no one but herself knew it was there.

She avoided evening gatherings at the Upper Assembly and promenades at the Pump Room that occupied Augusta and Elizabeth. Her brother was introduced to Tom Baldwin in whom he found a ready companion for riding and hunting which kept him entertained with visits to Holbourn, and the Wenthworths and Musgroves arrived in town in time for the anniversary party.

Everyone seemed to be happily occupied except Catherine whose only solace was to visit the excavation site when the workers were gone for the day and she was free to investigate what they had uncovered and document her observations in her notebook. Alone here, she could find peace and some level of tranquillity, but how was she to sustain it for the rest of the Season? Augusta and Charles would return to Dublin following the festivities, but she would remain in Bath with her mother and face the constant reminders of the regret that consumed her, knowing that soon she would face even greater pain when word finally arrived that Edward was officially engaged and she would be required to offer congratulations to the dubiously happy couple. She had to acknowledge that her wounds were self-inflicted because she would not listen to her own heart, and was unable to conquer her own fears and insecurities, and, while she felt she did not deserve him, she knew he did not deserve to marry without love; that it would be an unhappy outcome for them both.

Chapter 27

The workers at the site of the Roman ruins made progress that day, Catherine observed. A fragment of an outer wall had been removed revealing the remnants of a painted wall with an unusually vivid colour of Egyptian blue, a rare and expensive colour to produce in ancient times because the materials had to be imported from Egypt and manufactured using copper and other elements that were heated at very high temperatures to form a glassy material with Egyptian blue crystals in it. It was a remarkable find in a place so far removed from Rome and she opened her notebook to document the discovery so she could inform the foreman and the work crew to use extreme caution so as not to disturb this rare and valuable discovery.

She heard the sound of footsteps and wondered if the crew was returning to work, and looking up, she saw a figure emerge from the shadows. She raised the oil lantern the workmen had left behind to get a better look and caught her breath when she realised who was approaching her, Colonel Fitzwilliam.

"I was told by your mother that I might find you here," he said with a soft smile on his face. "She claims you spend a good deal too much time underground in the dirt and dust of this excavation site but I think it rather suits you for you seem completely in your element."

Catherine opened her mouth but nothing came out until finally she was able to collect herself and say, "I am very surprised to see you; I was told that no one knew your travel plans or whether to expect you here in Bath." She paused another moment, lowered her eyes, and finally faintly asked, "Are congratulations in order? I heard of late that you were likely engaged to be married. May I offer my good wishes for your happiness."

"Ah!" he exclaimed with a wide grin. "Good wishes is it? For my happiness? So you think I succumbed to the pressure of my family to give up my status as a single man and marry my cousin?"

"I understood your were enjoying an extended stay with your aunt and cousin, longer than usual it was said, and there was speculation that perhaps you had become engaged," she replied.

"That would be impossible," he responded. "Surely you, of all people, are aware that my heart belongs elsewhere and I would never enter into a loveless marriage to please my family."

"Then why the extended stay?" she asked.

"When I returned from Dublin I was afflicted with a

melancholy from which I could find no relief, as I am sure you must understand. I visited my father briefly but could not bear the vexation of listening to his admonitions to marry and expounding on the merits of taking a wealthy wife along with a beautiful mistress to balance out the qualities that might be missing in the one from the other. The 'business' of marriage, he claimed, has nothing to do with the heart and everything to do with enrichment of the family holdings; the heart would take care of itself in time. I was persuaded to make my annual visit to my aunt at Rosings Park and to extend my stay to give myself time to evaluate the merits of the proposition at hand as it was in everyone's best interests.

"On my way, I stopped to visit my cousin and his wife at Pemberley. I had last been there for the wedding of my cousin, Georgianna, and it was from there I traveled directly to Dublin with thoughts of playing the role of matchmaker for myself. Little did I know the difficulty I would encounter trying to persuade the brilliant, independent woman whom I met in Bath to accept my proposal of marriage, nor did I expect to lose my heart in the process.

"Spending time with my cousin and his wife was probably ill considered, for I was reminded of the happiness that can be shared by two people who genuinely love and respect each other. Mind you, theirs was not an easy courtship either. She viewed him as proud and vain while he considered her to be beneath his station in life. Despite all, they eventually came to discover they were perfectly matched, they balanced each other's temperaments, and are happily married.

"With that as my model for marital happiness, the time I

spent with Lady Catherine and my cousin exposed all of the shortcomings where amiability, intelligence, grace, and humour are completely lacking in either party, mother or daughter. I did extend my stay in hopes of turning a blind eye to their shortcomings as my father had advised, but it was to no avail. It was impossible to betray everything I hoped for and valued in a partner no matter how long I was there. Nothing could compel me to commit to a loveless marriage.

"When I received a letter from Darcy that they had just arrived in Bath and learned that you were in town, I made my excuses and rushed here to see you. You can have no doubt that my heart will always belong to you, Catherine, and that is what brought me here."

Catherine felt breathless with relief that he remained unattached and as she sought to regain her composure, she reached under her chemisette to touch the silk ribbon tied around her neck to ground herself. As her fingers idly stroked the ribbon his attention was drawn to it.

"What is that around your neck?" he asked. "I have never known you to wear any sort of adornment, even a silk ribbon."

Her hand froze as she replied, "It is something new that I have taken to wearing since I came to Bath," but she could not meet his gaze.

"May I ask if there is anything attached to your ribbon? Perhaps something that is precious to you? May I see?"

With that he gently touched the fingers at her neck to gather up the ribbon. As it emerged from her bodice, he held the antique silver button gifted by the Marquess of Sligo which he brought back for her from his journey to Connacht.

"Is this what I think it is? When last we met I suggested you attach a note saying this button represented 'The Heart of Edward Fitzwilliam'. Is that why you wear it so close to your own?"

"I cannot deny it," she replied softly. "I found I could not leave it behind when we travelled here and so I decided to conceal it," she admitted.

He gently lifted the button to his lips and kissed it. "Does this mean our hearts beat as one? Have you changed your mind? Will you reconsider and accept my hand and my heart?"

"Yes, Edward," she whispered.

"Make haste, my love. I must get you to your mother and ask for her permission before you have a chance to change your mind. I rode all night and half the day to get here in hopes that I could win your heart and I shall not have it snatched away again."

"I knew you would come to your senses at last," declared the dowager viscountess to her daughter. "You have restored my faith in your judgement and proven yourself to be a rational creature after all. What wonderful news has presented itself this day. When Colonel Fitzwilliam called seeking your whereabouts, it gave me hope that you would finally embrace this as a second chance and accept his proposal. Considering the eager look on his face and the alacrity in which he departed, I was certain that was his intention."

"The second son of an earl is an splendid conquest, my dear sister; you have done very well for yourself," enthused Augusta. "Very well, indeed, and such marvellous felicity to plan a wedding; it must be a grand affair and the highlight of the social season to be sure. Mamma and I will make all the arrangements as we know how you disdain the details of planning such an event; you need not trouble yourself on that account. It will be an elegant affair. Christ Church will be decorated as never before and dear Reverend Murry will be thrilled to officiate. Such felicity!"

"I am sorry to disappoint you but we intend to be married expeditiously here in Bath. We shall organise it as quickly as possible while Charles is still here and can walk me down the aisle."

"Very well then, as you wish, my dear," replied her mother. "You are quite right that it is convenient your brother and his wife are in town and how perfectly charming for them to both participate in your wedding since I am sure you will want your sister-in-law to stand as your witness."

"Indeed, what a charming idea, and you may count on me to make arrangements for new gowns as I know all the best shops and dress makers," chimed in Augusta.

"I will plan my own attire to suit my tastes, thank you. As to witnesses, Mr. Darcy will stand up for Colonel Fitzwilliam and I intend to ask his sister, Mrs. Baldwin to do the same for me."

"Mrs. Baldwin! Why Mrs. Baldwin?" demanded her mother. "You have only just become acquainted with her. Augusta seems a much better choice and she will be sorely disappointed if she is not included in the wedding party. After all, we will announce the wedding in the local paper and people will wonder at your choice."

"I regret that Augusta may be importuned, Mamma, but I have made up my mind on the subject and I have no concern for the opinions of strangers who happen to read the local society column. Edward is already in contact with the rector at St. Swithin's which is a lovely church here in Bath and will more than meet our needs for the small wedding we have in mind."

"St. Swithin's instead of the Abbey? It will not be nearly so elegant, and what of Colonel Fitzwilliam's family?" asked her mother. "Surely you will announce your plans to them and it will take time for them to arrange transport here."

"As I said, Mamma, we wish to marry as soon as possible. We will arrange to briefly visit his family after the ceremony and before we return to Ireland. He anticipates no objections by his family to his choice of wife considering they have been pressuring him to marry for some time now. There can be no concerns about my rank as daughter and sister of a viscount."

"Then you will return to Dublin right away? Such felicity!" Augusta chimed in. "We can plan a gala reception and invite all of Dublin society to Rathclare Hall to celebrate your nuptials. It will be a grand affair and you, of course, will be given the distinction of beginning the ball at the head of the line since it will be in your honour, and, knowing how you dislike that type of attention, you need only lead the first round of dancing."

"There shall be no large reception; it is not to my tastes and

Colonel Fitzwilliam has already been introduced to Dublin society during his last visit so it will be entirely unneccessary. We plan to take a wedding trip upon our arrival in Dublin and retrace the coastal route that Edward took south to Waterford and north along the western coast to Connacht where we will call on the Marquess of Sligo and his wife, so there is no need for you to organise any type of event."

Having quelled the ambitions of her mother and sister-in-law to turn her marriage into a public spectacle, they were left to focus their energies on the anniversary party for Sir Thomas and Lady Bertram.

Chapter 28

The anniversary party was a great success as reported in the society column of the Bath newspaper the next day, but the liveliest gossip revolved around the surprise announcement of the betrothal of The Honourable Miss Carteret, daughter of the Dowager Viscountess Dalrymple and sister to Viscount Dalrymple of Rathclare Hall in Dublin, to Colonel Fitzwilliam, with the ceremony to take place the following week at St. Swithin's.

Both ladies were gratified to read descriptions of their elegant attire along with the recognition that they set the standard of fashion in Bath for the Season and were much to be admired for their beauty and refinement. Elizabeth was well remembered as a doyenne of society when her father was alive and slipped comfortably into the role once again as the wife of a baronet rather than the daughter of one, and relished the recognition. Augusta enjoyed the acknowledgement of her elevated status as a viscountess to whom great deference was paid which suited her very well, although the dowager viscountess, who was used to being the focus of attention when in Bath found herself being overshadowed by her daughter-in-law.

While Augusta and Elizabeth regaled themselves the next day with the success of their party, the fashionable guests that attended, and the number of couples who took to the dance floor with Lady Bertram at the head of the line, neither was particularly amused by the level of attention given to the upcoming wedding which they considered to be less newsworthy than themselves.

"Really, I see no reason why a brief engagement and small wedding in an obscure church next week should receive more attention than the social event of the Season to celebrate the first anniversary of my marriage to Sir Thomas," complained Elizabeth. "It is not as though there will be much to write about in comparision as it certainly will not be a fashionable affair even with us in attendance."

"I agree entirely," replied Augusta. "If Catherine had chosen me for her bridal party, there would be far more to write about as far as elegance of attire and graciousness of manner. I do not understand the haste of their plan or why they wish to marry here rather than Dublin. It is her loss, however, and nothing to be done about it."

* ~ * ~ * ~ *

When Catherine walked down the aisle on the arm of her brother, the following week, she was attired in a simple, light taupe gown delicately embroidered in white with a small row of Irish lace trim on the bodice that matched the trim of her white veil. Details written of the event were limited to the small guest list, the style of dress worn by the bride, that the colonel was dressed in his regimental uniform, and the happy couple were to depart for Dublin right away.

The Darcys requested the privilege of organising a reception and dinner following the wedding of their cousin which was readily agreed upon. Georgianna Baldwin was elated to be included in the wedding party as a witness alongside her brother, Mr. Darcy. During the party, Mrs. Darcy approached Catherine and reminded her of the conversation they had the prior year regarding the traditional role of women and Georgianna's new found interest in science.

"Mrs. Baldwin is not only a wife but has emerged as a true partner to her husband as well," Elizabeth stated. "I admire the bond the two of you have formed based on your shared interests; it has been an inspiration for her. I remember a conversation we had during their engagement party when you asked Colonel Fitzwilliam about his thoughts on the need for more educational opportunities for women to which he asserted his agreement. Now that you are married, I am certain you two will be happily matched as equals which is as it should be. He will nurture and support your interests, you will enhance each others lives, and I wish you both great happiness. We hope you will visit us soon at Pemberley where you will always be welcome."

"I look forward to expanding our friendship, Mrs. Darcy,

and we will be delighted to visit you once we return from our wedding trip to Ireland. We intend to retrace the route he took on his recent visit; I am eager for the opportunity to explore the places he ventured to and the history he explored, but I know we will devise other travel plans as well that will surely include Pemberley."

* ~ * ~ * ~ *

"What shall I do in Bath all by myself?" complained the dowager viscountess. "I shall have to curtail my visit here now that all my family are returning to Ireland and that means discontinuing my treatment regimen which I have come to enjoy immensely. I shall have to travel home by myself and whom shall I travel with next year to Bath now that you are married?"

"Mamma, you must plan to stay in Bath and continue your treatments while Edward and I make a brief trip to his family's estate so he can introduce me to his father and brother. We will return to escort you back to Dublin before we depart on our wedding trip. We are in no rush to embark if it importunes you in any way."

"Well, I should think you would want to include me if you are to meet the family. Surely they will want to get acquainted with your mother?"

"Another time, Mamma. We would rather not disrupt your treatment plan and you will be better prepared to travel comfortably when we do embark for home. As to our plans for the following year, I cannot say, but I believe Mary Jameson would be much obliged to be considered as a travel companion and would greatly enjoy the entertainments that Bath has to offer."

"So long as she can manage her irrational impulses and romantic fantasies I shall consider it, but I do not wish to take responsibility for a young lady who cannot keep control of her own emotions, although I do believe she would benefit from the excellent social connections and entertainments we enjoy here, and I am sure her mother could spare her if I offered. Very well then, I shall take it under consideration."

Chapter 29

Catherine's apprehensions about meeting Edward's family weighed heavily on her mind but he was able to calm her anxiety and reassure her that all would be well, just as he was able to ease her self-consciousness and insecurities in private, and she found she was able to easily return his gentle, patient affection. She found a new level of self-confidence she had not anticipated and gradually developed more self-assurance socially. Even her mother noticed the change in her when they returned to Bath for the journey home.

"I must say, my dear, that marriage becomes you," commented her mother. "Your complexion is glowing, your eyes are brighter, and you even seem to smile more. I knew it would be so if you relinquished your stubborn promise to never marry and gave up your obstinant and headstrong ways. I am quite satisfied to see you are capable of amending your notions of independence in favour of a traditional role, that of a wife, and I am certain your father would be very pleased with you, as am I."

"I cannot say that I have given up my independence, Mamma, only that I have married a man who supports and encourages it. I shall never be as traditional as you may hope."

* ~ * ~ * ~ *

They spent time in Dublin arranging for their journey to Connacht which included visiting Dean Fitzgerald at Trinity to return some books and manuscripts. His delight and surprise at seeing them arrive together was as enthusiastic as it was ebullient.

"What joyful news to hear that you are married! I always knew it was meant to be even though you protested from a very young age that you would never compromise on that front, my dear. I worried for years that you would end up lonely and reclusive because of your determination to remain single and you have far too much to contribute to the world than you ever could achieve confined to your study and your visits to Trinity.

"I will admit that I formed a very high opinion of you, Colonel, from the first time we met and was certain you would be an excellent match for this dear lady. She needs adventure in her life and you are just the man to provide it. Who could not be impressed by your intrepid spirit, travelling to the hinterlands to discover the history of a pirate queen, and returning with proof of your adventure. Do you still keep that silver button safe, dear Catherine?"

"I do, Dean Fitzgerald. I have taken to wearing it around my neck on a ribbon and look forward to meeting the benefactor who gifted it to me, the Marquess of Sligo, very soon."

"Such felicity! An adventure already planned for your wedding trip. Very good news, but promise me you will visit when you return and share what you learn for I shall await you with eager anticipation. And what an ideal travel companion you will be wherever you venture with your unique language skills. You will never have need of an interpreter and no one will ever be able to cheat you," Dean Fitzgerald chortled.

"By the way, I have news of Duncan Woulff from colleagues in Rome that will interest you. It seems that when he made his way back he was apprehended by authorities for selling fraudulent antiques to some very affluent patrons and was scheduled to be taken to court for a trial. However, a wealthy patroness stepped in at the last minute to pay his substantial debts and have the charges dropped with the understanding that he was to remove himself from the antiquities business and find another means of income. Shortly thereafter, it was reported that he and the prosperous widow had married and were living at her villa in Porto Ercole on Monte Argentario overlooking the Mediterranean Sea in Tuscany. It seems she is a collector of paintings by Caravaggio who is buried there. Let us hope his interest in art and artifacts is no longer a priority in his life."

"Somehow it comes as no surprise that he would affix himself to a woman of wealth for he had great charm and personal attributes that attracted the attention of many women including some he met here in Dublin on whom he worked his wiles. It is safe to say he is an opportunist with a taste for luxury who is used to getting what he wants," commented Catherine.

"My dealings with him revealed him to be a scoundrel and a fortune hunter. His wife should watch her purse and keep a close eye on any young ladies within her orbit for he is not to be trusted," replied Colonel Fitzwilliam. "I am very happy you did not fall under his influence since you had known him from the past."

"Oh, he made an effort to open that door but I observed him enough in company to see through his artiface. I was never in danger."

At Catherine's insistance, they made their way from Trinity to the local pub, the Gerty Browne, to have a pint of the local brew. This time she need have no fear of scandalising her family by entering such an establishment since she was no longer a single woman and could go anywhere on the arm of her husband to enjoy all the music and poems and cheer such an establishment had to offer. She did not stand and make a recitation this time, but smiled at the thought that she could; she was finding that, strangely enough, smiles came more readily than ever before which greatly pleased her husband.

After the barmaid arrived to serve their pints, Catherine announced she wished to make a toast. "To Grace O'Malley, the pirate queen of Connacht, whose story inspired the matchmaker from Pemberley to visit Dublin in pursuit of a rather reluctant bride."

"To a woman who knows her own mind and is not afraid to

change it," laughed Edward. "It is true what you say, my dear. In you I recognised the same kind of uncompromising, intelligent, fiercely independent woman that Grace O'Malley must have been, and the more I learned of her, the more I knew I could never settle for anyone who was not her equal."

When they embarked on their honeymoon, Catherine and Edward travelled overland to the Wicklow Mountains since Edward was determined to see the view of the sea below before they made their way to the seaside town of Wicklow to board a ship that would take them to Waterford. There they visited the famous crystal manufacturing facility and visited the burial place of the Dearg Dur, a wronged woman who folklore claimed had turned into a vengeful vampire. Catherine brought flowers to honour her memory.

The trip to Connacht was exhilerating and, with the wind in her face, as they passed Hags Head at the southern end of the Cliffs of Moher, Catherine realised for the first time just how happy she was standing next to the man she had once rejected. Her fears and insecurities, her diffidence and reserve, all seemed to melt away as each day brought new experiences and prospects. She had existed in a trap of her own making for most of her life and was exceedingly grateful to the man who helped her escape. She never realised she had an appetite for adventure as it never occurred to her that marriage and adventure could coexist, or that harmony with another person who accepted her as she was, would be possible.

She spent most of her life defending her right to develop the gifts with which she was born and avoiding those aspects of life that caused her anxiety or threatened to deter her from the right to pursue her interests. She was caught between two worlds, her father's scholarly inclination to nurture her manifest gifts while her mother denigrated them and demanded she fit into the uneasy model that society dictated. She learned to defend herself with behaviour that protected her but also isolated her and now she found she no longer needed those barriers. She felt at ease for the first time in her life and embraced each day with wonder and enthusiasm.

When they reached Clare Island, she was delighted to discover the caretaker who regaled Edward and his companions with stories of Grace O'Malley, was still there to spin his yarns and provide a tour of the island and Granuaile's Castle. Her ability to converse in the Irish language earned his immediate admiration and respect; it also amplified his storytelling abilities. She was particularly intrigued with exploring the medieval paintings on the O'Malley family tomb and trying to ascertain when and whom may have created them. She decided she would have to return in search of clues and also make inquiries to her benefactor.

Edward had written ahead to the Marquess of Sligo to announce their travel plans and they had received an invitation to stay as guests at Westport House. The marquess who had been educated at Eton and Cambridge was fluent in French, having lived there for a period of time, and he greatly enjoyed conversing with Catherine in that language. They speculated about the history of the O'Malley tomb and the roof paintings but there was no definitive answer to be found. He gladly produced the small wooden box that contained the remaining two silver buttons and note presumed to be in Grace

O'Malley's handwriting that said 'The Heart of Philip Grenville'.

There was much discussion about Grenville and speculation about his family history and whether he was related to Sir Richard Grenville who had been a plantation owner in Munster briefly but was more well known as an adverturous seafarer. It was impossible to know but made for lively conversation as well as did the known encounter between Grace O'Malley and Queen Elizabeth which was of particular interest and Catherine became determined to access the original documents describing the meeting if they ever travelled to London and to share what she learned. On learning of her interest in visiting London to pursue the records, she and Edward were invited to visit the marquess at his London home in Marylebone where they intended to be in residence later in the year.

As it happened, the Marquess of Sligo was also well acquainted with Lord Byron, one of England's leading poets, whom he met during his Cambridge days, so there was much discussion about his influence on the Romantic movement and lengthy narrative poetry. The stimulation of these conversations was gratifying to both Catherine and Edward since they shared a love of poetry and began reading Byron's "Don Juan" to each other when they retired at night.

The wife of the marquess, Lady Hester, was a very pretty, cultured woman who, despite her young age, was very committed to overseeing the rennovations of Westport House and the extension of its gardens. She encouraged Catherine to explore the foundation of the building that was built on one of the O'Malley's fortresses as well as the remains of some of the other fortresses built by the O'Malley clan to maintain their control of the coastline. They were able to explore at their leisure and enjoy the rugged, wild coastline of Connacht and imagine the exploits of the famous pirate queen who reigned over ships and sailors to protect her family's fortunes and pass a legacy down to her descendants thanks to her astute negotiations.

* ~ * ~ * ~ *

"Where shall we go next, my love? Tell me your heart's desire," offered Edward.

They had retired for the night at Westport House having spent the day exploring ruins and engaging locals to share the folklore they knew about the famous pirate queen from two centuries past. The fact that Catherine spoke the Irish language opened doors and stories flowed wherever she raised the topic. Some stories were clearly confabulated but others remained consistent and Catherine took note of them all even though none could ever be corroborated.

They planned to return to Dublin via the route Edward had taken so she could see the prison where Tibbot Burke was once incarcerated, met his wife, and from where he was set free, thanks to the negotiations of his mother with Queen Elizabeth. He went on to become the first Viscount of Mayo the same year his mother, the rebellious pirate queen, and the celebrated English queen died. Catherine marvelled that the random story she chose to share with Edward in one of their early conversations when they first met in Bath, would lead her to this destination, travelling with a man she had sworn to never marry, and now loved beyond measure. It exceeded anything she could ever have imagined.

"We must check in on Mamma, of course, and suffer through any social events that Augusta is sure to organise on our behalf, or, should I say, her behalf, for she does love to play the grand hostess despite whatever wishes we may have. Still, you adapt so well to these affairs while I find them utterly disagreeable, especially when I am forced to be the centre of attention, and I shall have to rely on you to help me face it all with forebearance, despite the fact that I am importuned. You must be charming on my behalf while I shall try to persevere."

"I call that a fair bargain but I do believe you are not so aloof as you once were and mingle more easily with people than you used to do, so do not be alarmed by social commitments foisted upon us. They will be over soon enough and we shall be off on a new adventure. We have ready invitations in London from both our hosts here in Westport as well as the Darcys who have a house there as well. We shall be in demand there but in a more companionable environment. The question remains, what is your heart's desire? Where shall we travel to next?"

"Italy. I must see Italy. Rome, Florence, Venice, I want to see it all. And Greece, I long to visit Athens and the Parthenon. Oh, to see the temple of Athena, the goddess of war, would fulfill a dream I never dared to dream," enthused Catherine.

"Having read Homer's *Odysseus,* I can understand why you would be drawn to a Greek goddess who dons a helmet and carries a spear, someone fierce and independent, not unlike Grace O'Malley. I begin to understand you better with each day that passes."

"Imagine what I may discover there to share with Dean Fitzgerald. I believe if I am able to visit Italy and Greece, I shall be content forevermore," replied Catherine.

"Then that is my heart's desire, my love, to see you content and happy."

* ~ * ~ * ~ *

Edward conjured a travel scheme that exceeded anything Catherine could have hoped for. With the end of the Napoleonic Wars, travel through the European continent was much safer so he proposed they start in Luxembourg and travel by boat through the Confederation of the Rhine and then on to the Kingdom of Italy. It would require an extended travel itinerary and coordination of transportation resources, but he was ever adventurous and wanted his wife to see as much as possible of the world. Catherine marvelled at the prospect of such a journey and it was decided that he should hire a man servant and she a personal maid to help manage their packing, attire, and transport requirements during the trip.

When Birdie arrived to help prepare her for bed, she drew back the covers, brought out her night clothes, and began brushing her hair just as she had done since Catherine was a young girl.

"Birdie, what do you think of leaving Rathclare Park for an extended trip through Europe to Italy and then on to Greece? I shall need a personal maid and you are the person I trust most in the world to look after my affairs and take care of my needs. We shall be gone many months travelling by boat down the Rhine River and cross majestic mountains into Italy where we will visit Rome and Venice before travelling by sea to Greece. It will be an extraordinary journey and an opportunity of a lifetime for you. What do you think?"

"I am gobsmacked, Miss. I have never thought to travel anywhere further than Howth by the sea and though me Mam will miss me, she will not try to hold me back from such an adventure to be sure. Can you believe it, Miss? You and I travelling the world? 'Tis a wondrous thing to even consider and beyond anything I could ever dream.

"Just look at you, Miss. A married lady though you swore never to do so, with an amiable husband who wants to explore the world with you, and though you will have no need to speak the Gaelic during your travels, you will make fine use of all those other languages you know. What a wonder it will be to travel and meet new people in so many countries and be able to talk to all of them. Perhaps this is the reason the Lord gave you such gifts; now you will finally have the opportunity to put them to use.

"I always knew there was something special about you and look at yourself in the mirror there. You are not so gaunt as you used to be, you fill out your dresses more, and then there is the blush in your cheeks now, where your complexion used to be so sallow from too much staying indoors.

"Take my word for it, marriage becomes you, Miss. That journey by sea was just the thing you needed after spending so many years locked away in your study with your mam nipping at your heels to find a husband even though that was not your inclination and she knew it. Ah, how you battled her and held steadfast to your commitment to remain single despite her nagging. She thought you stubborn and headstrong and indeed you were, but once the right gentleman arrived on the scene and was patient enough to wait you out, well then, as the saying goes, 'what fills the eye fills the heart' and, in my opinion, your heart is very full, for which I for one am glad. After all, the only cure for love is marriage and it is love that caught you out. Mercy me, just wait until I tell me mam and the kitchen staff that I shall become a world traveller in service to my mistress. They will be gobsmacked to be sure."

What Birdie said was true, Catherine thought. There was an old Irish proverb, "Ceileann suil an ni na feiceann" or "the eye shuns what it does not see", and she had been guilty of blindness until she was finally able to see herself through Edward's eyes. "Is maith an scathan suil carad" or "a friend's eye is a good mirror" described her dear friend, her husband, the man who appreciated her as she was but also who she could be. Once the scales fell away, her life had opened up and she was flourishing; she would never be the same woman, withdrawn, remote, reserved. She was forever changed. As she gazed at her image in the mirror, she could not help but notice the face reflected back was fuller, the complexion rosier, the eyes brighter, and, for the very first time in her life, she realised that perhaps she was not so very plain after all.

The End

Acknowledgements

The following resources were used to create a vivid depiction
of Irish history during the life and times of Jane Austen.

How the Irish Saved Civilization by Thomas Cahill
The Rebels of Ireland by Edward Rutherford
The Mandrake Broom by Jess Wells
Classic Irish Proverbs by James O'Donnell
Irishcentral.com
Wikipedia

About the Author

Catherine Kelly Hemingway is a literary and visual artist focused on Austenesque novels and pastel portraiture. A retired marketing executive, Catherine debuted her first novel, The Matchmaker of Pemberley in 2023 followed by Pemberley to Dublin: A Matchmaker's Journey which released in 2024. Visits to Bath, Chawton, and Winchester rekindled her passion for the remarkable novels and life of Jane Austen. A monthly blog examines the personality dynamics of Austen's characters and how they reflect her own life's experience. If Catherine isn't writing, she is painting, and living out her philosophy to "play your part with a joyful heart, make your life a work of art."

www.catherinehemingway.com

Made in the USA
Las Vegas, NV
12 December 2024